W9-BBB-674

Dear Reader,

Have you ever known someone who loves restoring old things? It amazes me that instead of seeing a chair with a cracked leg and worn-out upholstery that's ready for the trash pile, they see possibility. Or maybe *you're* that person who loves taking vintage toys and antique furniture and making the old new again.

One of the things I enjoyed about writing *The Restoration Project* was exploring not only the fascinating process behind restoring a piece of antique furniture, but also being reminded on a more personal level, like Sadie, that furniture isn't the only thing that sometimes need to be restored.

If you think about it, there's probably someone in your life right now who always ends up rubbing you the wrong way. Someone you might even go out of your way to avoid. That person who needs a bit of grace. You probably know exactly who I'm talking about. Right? It's never easy to take that first step in restoring relationships. Especially if you feel like you're not the one at fault.

In most cases though, even with people, it sometimes takes a bit of sanding and polishing before you can find out exactly what's underneath. And as Sadie discovers, both in the restoration project she's working on and in relationships, you just might end up being surprised with what you find!

So sit back, relax, and get ready to enjoy another trip to the quaint town of Silver Peak with Sadie and her friends.

Best wishes,
Lisa Harris
writing as Carole Jefferson

Mysteries of Silver Peak

A Mountain of Mystery
Nobody's Safe
Silver Surprise
Wildfire
A Lode of Secrets
Time Will Tell
A Code of Honor
Empty Saddle
Reunion Dance
The Counterfeit Caper
A Blessing and a Curse
The Restoration Project

The Restoration Project

CAROLE JEFFERSON

Guideposts
New York

Mysteries of Silver Peak is a trademark of Guideposts.

Published by Guideposts Books & Inspirational Media
110 William Street
New York, New York 10038
Guideposts.org

Acknowledgments

Every attempt has been made to credit the sources of copyrighted material used in this book. If any such acknowledgment has been inadvertently omitted or miscredited, receipt of such information would be appreciated.

Cover and interior design by Müllerhaus
Cover art by Greg Copeland represented by Deborah Wolfe, Ltd.
Typeset by Aptara, Inc.

Printed and bound in the United States of America
10 9 8 7 6 5 4 3 2

Prologue

S.P.
4/21/22

Dear R,

I fear the end of my life is near, my friend. An officer was killed two blocks from my house last night on Main Street, and I feel certain they will find a way to tie it back to me even though I wasn't involved. This morning, my brother was arrested and taken in for questioning, and while they were unable to prove he was involved, I've been told they are now searching for me.

For too long, I have justified the two lives I live; I thought I could rationalize my involvement in the illegal ventures of our association by giving to various charities and needy families in our community, but even that isn't enough anymore. Perhaps I'm simply getting too old, but as lucrative as our new business has been—helping to quench the thirst of this state—I fear for my family, and the position I have put them in.

I have hidden the remaining balance I owe you—with an additional large bonus—in the usual place. My debt is paid. But for me, I fear my only option is to disappear. Please do not try to find me.

Sincerely,
L

1

SADIE SPEERS SCANNED THE WELL-MANICURED LAWN, PAST THE typical assortment of shoppers, collectors, antique dealers, and interior designers that always showed up at a high-end estate sale. Where had Roz gotten to now? The last time Sadie had seen her best friend, she was eyeing a set of blue-etched water tumblers on the far corner of the yard. Two dollars a glass might be a bargain, but today Sadie had been looking for a specific item she'd discovered in the classifieds of the *Silver Peak Sentinel*: a two-piece bedroom set from the late-nineteenth century for one of her regular antique clients, Marge Ruxton.

Brushing past a younger couple who were haggling over the price of a piece of art, Sadie finally spotted Roz's lanky figure a few feet ahead of her.

"I have a feeling Roscoe's going to disown me for bringing you here," Sadie said with a chuckle once she caught up to her.

Roz turned and shot her friend a wide grin, clutching a large floral tote filled with her purchases. Sadie had known Roz since their first day of kindergarten over a half century ago. Sadie's opposite in many ways, Roz towered over Sadie's five-foot-four frame by a good eight inches. While Sadie wore her thick salt-and-pepper hair short, Roz's gray hair framed her face in a longer, neat bob.

And yet it wasn't just their physical appearance that set them apart. Despite occasional dramatic moments, Roz tended to have more of a calm, collected nature, while Sadie's first tendency was to jump headfirst into things. But Sadie had always been convinced that those differences were a main factor in why their friendship had continued to blossom. She'd said it more than once over the years, but Roz was, without a doubt, the string to her kite who had helped her soar through life, especially through the difficult times.

"What did you find?" Sadie asked.

Roz held up a necklace that was nestled at the top of the bag. "I went ahead and bought eight of the glasses, but I also found this."

"It's gorgeous." The multicolored braided necklace would fit perfectly with Roz's collection of colorful bohemian clothes she often paired with lots of jewelry. Sadie's style was more utilitarian, favoring simpler clothes made for the Rocky Mountain climate and terrain like North Face vests, hiking boots in the winter, and Teva sandals in the summer.

"What about you?" Roz asked. "Were you able to snag that bedroom set for Marge?"

"Got it." Sadie gestured toward the house where James Abbott, the estate sale manager, had organized the majority of the furniture. "They'll deliver it to the shop later today."

"That's fantastic! I can't wait to see it. But before we leave, I need your advice on one last thing," Roz said. "I think I've found the perfect birthday present for Roscoe." She pulled Sadie to the far end of the yard to a table filled with board games and wooden puzzles.

"What do you think?"

"Wow." Roz had led her to a chess set that looked hand-carved and easily close to a hundred years old. Sadie picked up one of the dark cherrywood pieces from the chessboard with leather touches on the sides. "I think Roscoe would love this. But you'd better snatch it up. I'm surprised it hasn't already sold for that price."

"You should sell antiques or something," Roz joked. "I'll buy it now and meet you at the car."

While Roz made her way to the checkout counter, Sadie browsed through a table of mismatched collectibles another minute or two before heading back toward her car. On her way, a woman bumped into Sadie, dropping a box of books she was carrying in the process.

"Oh, I'm so sorry." The young woman, in a T-shirt and jeans, frowned as she glanced up at Sadie. "My mind's a million miles away, and I wasn't paying attention at all."

"No problem," Sadie said. "Looks like we have something in common." She bent down to help the woman pick up the scattered books. She reached for a copy of Louisa May Alcott's *Little Women*. Sadie picked up another book, knowing if she would have discovered these earlier, she'd have bought the entire collection. Beatrix Potter, Rudyard Kipling, Ray Bradbury, Jack London... While she loved all antiques, paper ephemera—books, ledgers, notebooks, and photographs—were some of her favorite antiques. "You have a terrific collection here," Sadie said. "There are a few of these that could be worth some real money."

The girl looked confused, as if unsure why Sadie would know this information.

"Sadie Speers," she said, and held out her hand. "Owner and proprietor of Silver Peak's Antique Mine shop."

The young woman shook her hand. "Ashley King," she said. "These books were my grandpa's."

Sadie put another book into the box. "Danny Solomon was your grandfather?"

"Yep." She tugged on the end of her ponytail. "He left me these books and a house in Silver Peak, actually. You might even know the house. I don't know much about it yet, but I was told that it's called the Brown . . . I forgot. Brown something or other."

"The Browning House?" Sadie asked, not really trying to mask her excitement.

The young woman's lips curled into a shy smile. "So you do know of it."

"Of course." Sadie grabbed another one of the books. "It's an important landmark in Silver Peak, a beautiful piece of history, although, sadly, it's been neglected over the years."

"That's what I heard," Ashley said.

Sadie set the book into the box, wondering if she could ask Ashley for a tour. Even run-down, the place had to be stunning inside. And while she'd never had the chance to take a peek, she'd always wanted to. From what she'd heard over the years—along with rumors of a few shady things that had taken place on the property—the house had inlaid parquet floors, ten-foot ceilings, built-in bookcases, and rumors of a genuine Van Briggle vintage fireplace with its famous jade-green tiles. If that's what it really was, Sadie didn't know a single antique collector who wouldn't jump at the chance to see one of those fireplaces made by the pottery luminary.

"If you're into antiques, you wouldn't happen know anything about old houses, would you?" Ashley balanced the box against her hip. "I've been told the house isn't worth much, but if there are things worth restoring…things that would increase the value of the house…"

"I'd love to take a look," Sadie said. "I wouldn't pass up the opportunity. I'm honored that you'd ask."

Ashley let out an audible sigh. "That would be wonderful. Then please—if you're sure you don't mind—feel free to stop by anytime. I'll be there for the next week or so getting it ready to sell. I could use all the help I can get."

"I'll definitely stop by," Sadie said. She rummaged through her purse and pulled out a business card, which she then handed to Ashley. "In case you need anything in the meantime."

"Thanks so much," Ashley said. "I'll see you soon." She slipped back into the crowd, and a moment later, Sadie walked to her car, where Roz was just arriving.

"Find anything else?" Roz asked, carrying the boxed chess set in her arms.

Sadie unlocked her red Chevy Tahoe, ready for the hour-long drive back to Silver Peak. "No, but I just met Danny Solomon's granddaughter."

"Poor girl. These estate sales are always difficult for the family." Roz slid the box carrying the chess set into the backseat, then climbed into the passenger side to sit beside Sadie.

Sadie put the car in reverse, then pulled out of the parking lot. "He left her the Browning House."

"That magnificent old corner house on Washington Avenue?"

"Yes, that's the one. I've always wanted to see inside it," Sadie said, not even trying to contain her grin. "She asked if I wanted to stop by and give her some advice on what might be of value in the house."

Roz laughed as they turned onto the freeway. "*If* you wanted to?"

"That's what I thought." Sadie let out a chuckle as she pulled away from the curb. "There's no way I'd pass up an opportunity to see if that house really has an authentic Van Briggle fireplace."

"I wouldn't mind taking a peek inside that house either," Roz said. "Did I ever tell you that my grandmother knew Anne Van Briggle when she lived in Colorado Springs?"

"Really?"

"She even owned a vase made by them. I'm not sure what happened to it, but it was supposedly worth quite a lot."

"Speaking of valuable things, how are you feeling about the chess set?"

Roz glanced at her watch. "I'm so excited. I think Roscoe is going to love it. It will be so fun to present it to him at his party tonight. He already opened some presents this morning at breakfast, so this will be a real surprise. And I'm guessing he'll want to start up a game right then and there."

"A little chess tournament among friends? I'm in," Sadie said. "And I've got a few tricks up my sleeve..."

"Oh, you're not the only one. Roscoe's been playing against the computer for years, so he'll be tough to beat."

Sadie laughed. "Then he might just have an edge. The only computer game I play is 'who can make the best bid on eBay?'"

"And nobody's better at that than you, my friend."

Later that evening, after enjoying a delicious dinner at Sophia's with Edwin and the Putnams, Sadie helped Roz set up dessert in the living room of Roscoe and Roz's cozy cottage. She set a plate of chocolate cupcakes with raspberry filling onto the living-room sideboard. Beside it, a carafe of coffee permeated the air with its heady aroma. She eyed one of the cupcakes, which Roz had picked up from Maggie at the Market. It was tempting to try one, but she wasn't sure she should indulge after eating one too many slices of pizza.

Sadie sat down beside Edwin on the blue-and-white-checkered couch, thankful, not for the first time, for how God had brought him back into her life. Long before she met her husband, T.R., she had been going steady with Edwin. In fact, she really couldn't remember a time she hadn't known him. But things changed, as they often do. Edwin ended up leaving Silver Peak in order to pursue a career as a circuit judge in Chicago.

Now, all these years later, things had once again completely changed. T.R. had passed away, and Edwin had returned to Silver Peak following his retirement, eventually becoming the mayor of their small mountain town. She hadn't expected a second chance at love, but that's exactly what she'd been given with Edwin.

She glanced at Edwin, admiring as always his distinguished, powerful build, with his attractive steel-gray hair and twinkling blue eyes. Tonight he was dress casually in a navy blue crew-neck sweater and khaki pants.

"Do you know what's happened to my wife?" Roscoe's gaze shifted toward the hallway. He'd traded in the casual work attire he typically wore at his hardware store, Putnam & Sons, for a smart-looking button-up shirt and nice jeans for the occasion.

"It's never wise to ask too many questions on your birthday, Roscoe," Edwin advised with a grin.

"You're probably right. Especially when it comes to Roz." Roscoe chuckled as he sat down across from them on an overstuffed chair.

Before one of the men could comment further, Roz entered the living room, holding a neatly wrapped package in silver and white paper. "I have a surprise for you, Roscoe."

Roscoe shot his wife a pleased and questioning look. He slipped off the wrapping paper, pulled the chess set out of the box, and set it in his lap. "Roz, this is something else. Where in the world did you find it?"

"Do you like it?" Roz sat down on the arm of the chair, beaming. "I picked it up at the estate sale Sadie and I went to today. Sadie thinks it's at least a hundred years old."

"Like it? I love it." He leaned in and kissed her, and Roz let out a contented sigh.

"I thought you would."

Roscoe turned his attention back to the set. He ran his finger along the intricate carvings on its side. "I've never seen anything quite like this."

Sadie nodded as Roz pulled on the handle of a small drawer and started pulling out the chess pieces. "Look at this... Do you see these marks along the edges?"

"Yeah," Roscoe said, leaning in closer. "They look like some sort of inscription."

Now all four of them were leaning forward to get a closer look. Sadie ran her finger across the markings. In contrast to the set's dark wood, the thin swirling design that flowed around the edges of the board was lighter in color. The markings didn't seem uniform enough to be decorative, but neither was she able to read them as if they were supposed to have any kind of order to them.

"It could be some sort of code," Sadie suggested, half-kidding.

"I don't know about that, but I do know what I'm going to do with this chess set—after we all play a few rounds tonight, that is," Roscoe said.

"Oh? What's the plan?" Roz asked, catching eyes with Sadie and smiling at their prediction that Roscoe would want to play tonight.

"I'm going to set it up in the store for customers to play." He put the chessboard onto the coffee table and started setting up the pieces.

"Perfect!" Roz clapped her hands eagerly. "It will certainly add to the Americana feel of the place."

Putnam & Sons was located next to Sadie's antique shop, and Roz was right: Her husband's quaint hardware store was a supreme example of vanishing Americana. Much like the general stores of generations past, it was the kind of place where people came for advice and conversation as well as goods, and Roscoe happily provided both. He stocked a dizzying array of parts and pieces that provided just about anything a customer needed for repairs, plumbing, or gardening. The chessboard would be a natural fit.

"I love that idea," Sadie said. "Which reminds me, Roscoe. I need to drop by in the morning to see about getting the supplies I need to restore a bedroom set I bought today. I'm hoping your shop will have most of what I need so I don't have to make a trip into Denver anytime soon."

"Door's always open, Sadie." He smiled. "But in the meantime, care to take me on?"

"I thought you'd never ask," Sadie teased.

"Speaking of renovations," Edwin said, pouring himself a mug of decaf coffee from the sidebar before grabbing one of the cupcakes. He settled on the couch, while Sadie and Roscoe set up the chess pieces, and set his mug on the coffee table. "A woman came in to the town hall today with her uncle and the deed to the old Browning House."

"Someone actually bought that place?" Roscoe asked, taking the first move.

"No, it was willed to her," Edwin said.

"I met her today, actually," Sadie said. "At the estate sale." Sadie moved a pawn forward to the center, relying on her memory to copy the plays her father had taught her years ago. "I've always found it sad that the place has been completely let go. But I guess that's what happens when you have one bad renter after another."

"Unfortunately that's what Ashley discovered," Edwin said. "She wanted to know if the city had money in its budget to restore historical houses, as the Browning House was built in the late eighteen hundreds in the middle of the silver boom. Of course, I had to tell her that there aren't any funds specifically for that, although there are a number of tax breaks and incentives offered."

"She asked me if I would take a look at the inside of the house. See if there's anything worth restoring."

Sadie waited her turn, then moved her knight forward into position. In the late 1800s, Silver Peak had been a boomtown, driven by the silver mines that surrounded the area. People had become vastly wealthy overnight and built large Victorian-style houses around town until the mines finally stopped producing. Over the years, various individuals had restored a good number of the houses and now used them as personal residences or homey bed-and-breakfasts.

They'd managed to raise money to restore the town's historic opera house, which had been slated for demolition, where numerous luminaries from Sarah Bernhardt to Oscar Wilde to Mark Twain had graced the stage back in the town's mining heyday, but Edwin was right. The town's budget simply wasn't able to include renovating many of its other historical properties.

"I got the impression she was in need of cash," Edwin said, "but the problem is, I'm not sure who would want to buy the place in the condition it's in even with some of its features restored."

"Still," Sadie said, making her next move, "with some hard work and elbow grease, the place could be stunning."

"I wonder, though, if a renovation would be enough to bring in a buyer," Roz said. "Not that I'm superstitious or anything, but you've heard the rumors about that place. One of the owners was supposedly murdered in the living room."

"Which might be one explanation why no one has ever bought the house," Sadie said.

"Surely you're not afraid of those rumors behind the Browning House ghost." Roscoe looked up and shot Sadie a grin.

"Not at all. But maybe you should be. Afraid, I mean." Sadie couldn't help the feeling of triumph that surged in her as she caught Roscoe's gaze. "Checkmate!"

Sadie was still in good spirits the next day when she pulled onto Main Street and parked in front of the Antique Mine. Before the long walk she took every morning with Hank—her golden retriever named after the one and only Hank Williams—she'd had her devotional time, then made a list of everything she needed from Putnam & Sons to refurbish Marge's bedroom set. Marge had told her she would come by later today, so Sadie planned to clean the wood this morning before she arrived.

Roscoe and Roz arrived a minute behind Sadie in Roscoe's dark red pickup.

"You know I'm going to have to call for a rematch," Roscoe called as the vehicle pulled to a stop.

Sadie laughed. "I expected as much."

After the couple exited the pickup, Sadie and Roz hugged, then waited on the sidewalk while Roscoe proceeded to unlock the front of his store. A second later, he froze in the doorway.

"Roscoe?" Roz asked, moving in behind her husband. "What's wrong?"

"Someone broke in." Roscoe walked through the door, then moved aside, allowing the two of them to step into the store beside him. "The front door doesn't look messed with, but I can assure you that *those* weren't here when I closed up last night."

Sadie followed Roscoe's gaze and was shocked by what she saw. A row of muddy footprints crossed the hardware store's floor.

2

Sadie walked past Roz across the wood flooring of Putnam & Sons, then stopped in front of the muddy footprints. "You said there's no sign someone broke in from the front?"

"Not that I can tell. There's no broken glass. No scratch marks on the handle. Nothing obvious that would suggest a break-in."

"Except for these muddy footprints," Roz pointed out.

"What about the back door?" Sadie asked, but Roscoe had flipped on one of the lights and was already striding back to check the door that led to a narrow alley behind the store.

"This doesn't make any sense," Roscoe said a moment later. He turned around to face Sadie and Roz, who stood waiting in the middle of the store. "Both doors were locked, and I can't see any signs of a forced entry."

"Someone might have tracked the mud in yesterday before closing time," Sadie said, throwing out what seemed to her an obvious explanation.

Roscoe shook his head. "These footprints definitely weren't here when I locked up. I'm sure of that."

Sadie searched for another way to interpret the evidence. "Maybe one of your customers who came in at the end of the day…"

"That's not possible." Roscoe ran a hand over his balding head. "Ricky's been mopping the floors every night before I lock up, and last night was no exception."

"Who's Ricky?" Sadie asked, thinking she knew all Roscoe's employees.

"You'd probably recognize him if you saw him. He's a high school student who was looking for an after-school job a few months back." He gestured at Roz. "I didn't think I needed the extra help at the time, but I'll admit it's been worth it. He helps with stocking the shelves and keeping the place clean. And like I just said, one of his jobs is to sweep and mop the floor every day after closing."

"Maybe he got distracted and forgot yesterday?" Roz suggested, trying, like Sadie, to come up with something to explain away the muddy footprints in the middle of Roscoe's store. "You could have been thinking about our dinner plans and your birthday...It would have been perfectly normal to have missed something."

"But I didn't." Roscoe's voice rose a notch. "The last thing I do before leaving every night is to make sure everything is ready for the next day. My routine is exactly the same. I make my rounds, check to ensure any new inventory has been stocked, lock up the cash drawer, double-check the safe, turn out the lights, and make sure the front and back doors are locked. It's the same routine every night. I would have noticed."

Sadie wasn't surprised at his insistence. Roscoe was not only one of the most generous men she knew, he was also extremely conscientious and methodical. If he said he'd checked the store before locking up, she believed him.

"So whoever broke in must have had a key," Sadie said.

"Either that or they've got really good lock-picking skills," Roscoe said, then shook his head thoughtfully. "My assistant's the only one with a key, and he's out of town for the week on vacation. Fishing a hundred miles from here."

"You need to call Sheriff Slattery," Roz said. A hint of worry had crept into her voice.

"I'm not sure a few muddy footprints warrant a call to the authorities," Roscoe said. But it was clear he was worried as well.

Sadie frowned, her gaze still fixated on the footprints. "He'll probably want to know whether anything was taken."

Roscoe shrugged. "Nothing's messed up from what I can tell, though I won't be able to determine that for sure without doing an inventory."

Sadie watched as Roscoe returned to the front door, stopped in front of it, turned the handle, then paused. He ran his finger up the door frame, pausing near the top. He then moved slowly along the storefront, past the front window where a display was set up of power tools and other miscellaneous items that could be found in the store.

"What are you looking for?" Roz asked.

"Just trying to understand how someone managed to break into my shop without leaving any obvious signs. There are no broken windows, no apparent marks on the door handle... nothing."

Roz crossed the floor, then rested her hand on her husband's arm. "What are you thinking, Roscoe?"

"Nothing." He flipped on the rest of the overhead fluorescent lights, which slowly *plink*ed and eventually flickered on to full brightness, revealing the store's pressed-tin ceiling. "I need to open the store. I'll have customers coming any moment and..."

"That's not what I mean, Roscoe. I know that look in your eye, and I know what you mean when you say '*nothing*.' What's wrong?"

Sadie stood silently, watching the interaction between husband and wife. Clearly the situation had upset both of them.

"Well..." Roscoe pulled his phone from his back pocket and took a couple of photos of the footprints. "The thing is, there have been a few other... strange things happening around the store..."

"Strange things?" Roz interrupted. "What are you talking about, Roscoe?"

"I'm sure it's nothing. That's why I haven't mentioned it to you. I've just chalked them up to clerical mistakes."

"But now? This is no clerical mistake," Roz said.

He turned to face her. "I know. Which is why I can't help but wonder if I'm missing something."

"Like what?" Sadie asked.

Roscoe looked to Sadie, then back to Roz where they stood beside a row of fishing supplies. "Over the past couple of weeks, I've noticed small discrepancies in the inventory. There were also some things that seemed to have been moved around on the shelves, which I knew had been organized."

"So it *is* more than just the muddy footprints," Sadie said, a sliver of unease now growing inside her. She proceeded with caution. "You said Tom has a key. What about Ricky?"

Roscoe nodded hesitantly. "Normally he doesn't have access to the key, but a couple of weeks ago, I had him lock up for me one evening."

"Did he give the key back?" Roz asked.

"Yes, but I suppose he could have had the key copied. I mean, he could have even done that right here." Roscoe gestured to the key-duplicating machine near the front of the store. He turned to face his wife and Sadie again. "But it would take a lot to convince me that Ricky is a thief. That is, if anything's even been stolen. He's a good kid. He's never given me any kind of problems, although..."

"What is it?" Roz pressed.

"Two days ago, I found a note in the trash for a parent-teacher conference for Ricky. It had something to do with academic probation."

"So he's having problems at school?" Sadie asked.

"I tried to ask him about it, but he told me it was nothing. He'd gotten behind in a class, and his teacher was worried. I suggested cutting back on his hours here at the store so he could study more, but he assured me he would make up the classwork. The bottom line is, just because he's struggling in a class doesn't mean he's a thief."

Sadie agreed with him there. She could see the conflict in Roscoe's eyes. Roscoe was the oldest of eight children. He'd grown up poor on a farm in Kansas, and he'd quit school at sixteen to work for the railroad so he could help to provide for his family. Not having a high school diploma, though, had never stopped him. When Roscoe's elderly cousin decided the Silver Peak winters had gotten too cold for his bones, Roscoe had stepped in and had run the store ever since. Helping out a young man in the community who needed a job was simply part of who Roscoe was.

"It is possible," Sadie began, trying to put the pieces together, "that he started taking a few items from the store. Nothing substantial, but enough to sell for some extra cash, thinking you wouldn't notice."

"But that's what's so strange. I went through the inventory a few days ago to see exactly what was missing."

"And?" Sadie prodded.

"The amount of things taken doesn't even total a hundred dollars. If Ricky—or whoever—needed money and is breaking in and stealing things, there are plenty of items here worth a whole lot more than a handful of flashlights and screwdrivers."

"I agree it doesn't make sense, but I still think you should call the sheriff and ask him to come check things out," Roz said. "I also think you need to have a talk with Ricky. I know you like him, but that doesn't mean he isn't somehow involved in this... whatever *this* is."

"But what am I supposed to say?" Roscoe asked. "I can't accuse the boy of stealing. All we know for sure is that there are muddy footprints in my store, and that a few things are missing. It's even possible I just made a mistake or two on an order form."

"You don't have to accuse him of anything," Sadie said. "Perhaps ask him about the missing inventory. Ask if he's noticed any discrepancies while he's been stocking items."

Roscoe rubbed the top of his head and frowned. "I could do that when he comes back to work, but I got a message from him last night. He won't be able to come in for the next few days. He had to go into Denver with his mom."

Roz looked at Sadie. "Now, there's some interesting timing. A bunch of stuff goes missing at the store, then a break-in, which happens to be the same morning he goes out of town?"

"It's not like he didn't just show up for work. He let me know." Roscoe shook his head. "Do you really think he'd do that if he was guilty?"

Roz shrugged. "I have no idea, but it still seems a bit off to me."

"It wasn't Ricky," Roscoe insisted. "If Ricky needed some extra money, he would have just asked me. I'm sure of that."

"Do you know his family?" Sadie asked.

"Not well," Roscoe admitted. "He lives with his mom outside of town, but he's never spoken much about her. I've only met her once. I know that they struggle somewhat to make ends meet, which is why he needed this job. He had a letter of recommendation from one of his teachers. That was enough for me."

"Okay, so if it's not Ricky, then who?" Roz said.

"I don't know, Roz. I just don't know."

Roz squeezed her husband's hand. "Promise me you'll go talk to the sheriff. Let him look into this. It'll make me feel better. Even if the missing items turn out to be nothing more than a mix-up with your inventory, at least we'll know."

"Roz is right," Sadie said. "It's worth calling Mac and letting him make the decision on whether or not to follow up on this."

Sadie caught the conflict in Roscoe's eyes. Normally she didn't like butting in to other people's business, but ignoring the situation wasn't going to make it go away.

"Fine. But I think I'll go over there and talk to him directly." Roscoe shoved his hands into his jacket pockets. "Do you mind watching the store until I get back, honey? Shouldn't take me long."

"Of course not," Roz said.

As soon as the front door clicked shut, Sadie turned to her friend. "You okay?"

"I don't know. This whole thing is a little unsettling. All I really know is that these footprints didn't just appear out of nowhere, unless we're ready to look into the possibility that a ghost has been pilfering through the inventory after hours."

The image brought an automatic smile to Sadie's lips, but from the look on her friend's face, Roz wasn't amused.

"That might be one explanation for the mysterious footprints," Sadie said, "but let's hope the true answer will end up being less spooky."

3

A WHILE LATER, WITH ROZ RIGHT BEHIND HER, SADIE UNLOCKED the front door to the Antique Mine. They had finally received assurances from Roscoe that Sheriff Mac Slattery had agreed to look into the situation. With nothing else they could do about it for the moment, Roz had asked Sadie to show her the bedroom set she'd arranged to have delivered while Roz had been shopping at the estate sale.

The bell above the door jangled as Sadie opened up the shop and Roz followed her inside. Sadie weaved her way through the store, running her hand across the top of a French Louis XV–style sideboard she'd picked up at a recent estate sale, past a pair of medieval-style tapestry seats, and the Royal Doulton figurines she'd arranged in a vintage curio cabinet.

While she'd spent the majority of her sixty-two years teaching business and history in the quaint mountain town of Silver Peak, she'd always had a love for antiques. Which was why, when she retired from teaching, she'd decided to open the Antique Mine in a former dressmaker's shop along Main Street. Trading educating students and late nights grading papers for combing estate sales and restoring antiques had turned out to be the perfect fit for her retirement years.

Now, a full decade later, Sadie was proud that the Antique Mine had built a reputation not only for having a fantastic selection of treasures from the past, but also for its competitive prices. Sadie tried hard to ensure that the store was always filled with a variety of antique furniture, along with shelves and armoires that held unique vintage and antique items that continuously cycled through the shop.

She looked around at her treasure trove of items, which included everything from vintage toys, to high-quality antique furniture, to Victorian-era treasures. There were also a few personal favorites she held on to, like the antique mahogany desk with a locking glass display case where she kept "smalls," smaller, valuable items that could easily be pocketed if not kept tucked away, and the old-style brass cash register that looked like a typewriter. As far as she could tell, though, from a quick inspection, everything looked exactly as it had when she'd left the evening before.

Sadie took her supplies into the back room and set the items on a large workbench. It was the perfect setup, as the room was big enough that she could do her refurbishing in the shop between customers. Her current project was Marge Ruxton's bedroom set.

"What do you think?" Sadie asked.

The mahogany piece was composed of a beautifully carved full-size headboard and footboard, as well as a marble-topped dresser with a mirror. While the marble was in good condition, the rich wood needed to be completely refurbished.

To Sadie's surprise, instead of sharing her excitement, Roz's brow puckered in concern. "Are you sure about this?"

"What do you mean?" Sadie asked.

Roz sighed. "To my eyes, anyway, the set looks like it's in pretty bad shape. And you know Marge..."

Sadie hesitated, knowing that Marge was the real issue behind her friend's concern.

Marge Ruxton was a frequent customer of Sadie's, as well as a long-term resident of Silver Peak. And while she and Sadie were fine acquaintances and both even attended Campfire Chapel, the woman did have a habit of getting under Sadie's skin. No matter how many projects Marge brought Sadie's way, the woman never seemed to be satisfied with her efforts. And more than likely, this bedroom set wouldn't be an exception.

But Sadie had already decided she couldn't worry about Marge. Or the condition of the furniture, for that matter. While some might look at the bedroom set and consider donating it to the local thrift shop, or even discarding it altogether, Sadie saw the restoration of this piece as a challenge she relished taking on. In the eighteenth century, the process of French polishing—a process that gave the wood a very high glossy surface—had become prominent, particularly with mahogany and other expensive woods. Sadie had completed the process a few times, and while the procedure was labor-intensive, she always enjoyed a challenge...even if it meant having to deal with Marge as well.

"In spite of my hesitations over the project, I can see that gleam in your eyes," Roz teased.

"What gleam?" Sadie asked.

"The gleam that tells me you're going to enjoy every minute of this restoration, regardless of Marge."

"You got me." Sadie laughed, breaking some of the tension in the room as she finished organizing the supplies she'd just bought.

"I can imagine exactly what this is going to look like when I'm done, and it's going to be stunning."

She knew it would be time-consuming, but her part-time employee, Julie, worked throughout the week, giving Sadie lots of time to escape to the back workroom.

The front bell jingled as Sadie turned around. "Oh, I didn't lock the door, and the store doesn't open for another hour." Sadie groaned.

"I bet that's her," Roz whispered.

Sadie pressed her lips together, hoping Roz was wrong. She'd planned to at least clean the furniture before Marge saw it for the first time.

"Sadie? Sadie, are you here?"

Sadie swallowed hard as she slipped out of the back room. But Roz was right. Marge was weaving her way through the displays of antiques toward the back of the store.

"Hi, Marge. How are you?"

"Sadie... Roz... I'm fine, thank you. I know I'm early, but after your call yesterday afternoon, I simply couldn't wait to see what you found."

Sadie hesitated, trying to shove aside any preconceived judgments toward the normally prickly woman. "As I told you on the phone, while it's exactly what you said you wanted, it's not in the best shape. But don't worry, I have no doubt that once I'm finished with it, you will hardly be able to tell it's over a century old."

Marge bustled into the back room with Sadie, then stopped short in front of the furniture.

Sadie glanced at Roz. "What do you think, Marge?"

Marge set her handbag on Sadie's workbench and cast an appraising eye on the furniture. She ran her perfectly manicured fingertips across the top of the headboard, then brushed off the layer of dust that had gathered on her hand. "You're right. It's in pretty bad condition."

"Restoring a bedroom set like this is time-consuming."

"How time-consuming?" Marge asked.

"I'll first need to prepare the wood, then fill the grain to create a mirror-flat surface. After that, I'll apply the shellac thick enough to protect the wood, remove any oil from the surface, then continue the steps of leveling and applying more shellac..."

"There is something you need to know." Marge pressed her hands against her ample hips. "I need it finished in two weeks."

"Two weeks?" Sadie ignored Roz's pointed *I-tried-to-warn-you* look.

"When I first spoke to you about the project," Marge said, "I was expecting my family to come for a visit late next month. But my sister called me last night to say that there was a problem with that schedule. They're coming the end of next week instead."

"The end of next week?"

"And they're bringing my mother," Marge rushed on, "which means I have to finish redoing the guest room *before* they arrive." She sucked in a deep breath. "Sadie, I was hoping—no, I am *needing*—this bedroom set to be finished by then."

Sadie opened her mouth to speak, then closed it again. That didn't even give her two weeks. She wasn't sure the restoration was even possible in that length of time. "I can't make any promises, but I'll certainly do my best."

Marge let out a huff of air. "I hope so, because I'm counting on you."

The bell on the front door jingled again.

"I can't stay," Marge said, picking up her handbag. "Lanford's driving me to Denver today to pick out the new wallpaper for the guest room. I'll stop by in a day or two and see what progress you've made."

All Sadie could do was force a smile. "Fantastic, Marge. I'll see you soon, then."

Sadie and Roz followed Marge back into the store. Sheriff Slattery waited at the front.

"Nice to see you this morning, Marge," Mac said.

Marge nodded as she passed the lawman on her way out.

"Good morning, ladies. I wasn't sure if you were open yet, Sadie." Mac took off his hat and passed it back and forth between his hands.

"Morning, Mac. I'm not. Not technically, anyway."

"But I'm glad you stopped by." Roz took a step forward. "I know Roscoe went by to see you a little while ago, but I have to admit, I'm concerned about what might be going on at the store."

"So am I. Which is why I'm here. I wanted to stop by and ask a few questions—to you in particular, Sadie—about what's going on."

"To me? I don't understand," Sadie said.

"You might have heard something about it on the news. Over the past couple of months, a number of nearby towns have had to deal with a ring of thieves who have been breaking into stores." Mac ran the brim of his hat through his fingers. "And while I don't know if there's any connection to what is happening at Putnam & Sons, neither can I dismiss the possibility that they've decided to hit our town."

"I did read about them," Sadie said. "But I thought they caught whoever was behind the thefts."

"Turns out they arrested the wrong suspects, so they're still at it," Mac said. "Which is why, with you next door to Roscoe's shop, Sadie, I wanted to ask if you'd seen anything that struck you as strange over the past few weeks."

"Strange?" Roz asked. "Like what?"

"Anything out of the ordinary, including any unusual people. Anyone who stood out or struck you as odd or out of place. There's a good chance the thieves case their victims' shops before breaking in."

Sadie gripped the top rail of a high-back chair next to her. "No, I can't recall anyone or anything strange lately."

There had been a slew of the typical tourists who came through Silver Peak on a regular basis: retired couples, families with young children, locals... But nothing she could recall that seemed out of the ordinary.

"Anything missing from your shop?" the sheriff asked.

Sadie shook her head. "No, but I admit it's been a little while since I've done a thorough check."

The sheriff set his hat back on his head. "I'll be going around asking the other businesses in town the same questions in order to rule out some kind of pattern, but if both of you would let me know if you notice anything unusual, I'd appreciate it."

"And in the meantime?" Roz asked.

"I checked the doors and windows next door and couldn't find any signs of a break-in, including the locks being picked, which would definitely leave a mark. That means whoever is coming and going, as Roscoe believes is happening, must have gained access to a key. I've suggested the first thing he should do is change the locks on the front and back doors."

"That's a good idea," Roz said.

Sadie glanced at Roz as the sheriff said good-bye, then slipped out the front door a moment later, the bell jingling at his departure. "Roz? You okay?"

"I'm fine, I suppose. I just don't like the thought of someone breaking into the store. It makes me feel...vulnerable."

"I agree completely. But I also know that the sheriff will get to the bottom of this."

"I know." From the look on Roz's face, though, her friend wasn't convinced. "Anyway, I'd better get going. I told Roscoe I'd help him in the store today."

"And I suppose I need to get to work on that bedroom set, with Marge's deadline looming. Thankfully, Julie will be here in about an hour to watch the shop." Sadie started to open the door for Roz, then paused. "Of course, there is one other thing I'd like to do in the next day or two."

"What's that?" Roz asked.

"Stop by the Browning House."

Roz's eyes twinkled from behind her glasses. "That Van Briggle fireplace."

Sadie laughed. "Exactly."

"I'd still like to go with you, if you want," Roz offered. "What about tomorrow morning before you open?"

"I'd love that." Sadie's smile faded. "And in the meantime, we'll hope the sheriff discovers what's going on."

Roz paused before heading out the door. "Do you think I'm overreacting by worrying?"

"Not at all." Sadie felt a slight shiver creep up her spine as Roz left and the door clicked shut.

4

Friday morning, Sadie and Roz met in front of the Antique Mine an hour before the shop was to open, then walked together toward the Browning House. Sadie breathed in deeply, relishing the crisp morning air. She loved this time of year, when the trees turned from their normal lush green to the wide display of orange and yellow hues of fall. And on top of that, they were also enjoying unseasonably warm temperatures that had managed to hang on over the past week, making the weather perfect for being outside.

"Did you make any progress on the bedroom set yesterday?" Roz said, as they turned onto Washington Avenue.

"I've cleaned it and got a big chunk of the sanding process done. I'm just hoping I can meet Marge's time frame. It's going to be tight. Very tight."

"You could always put her to work," Roz suggested.

Sadie chuckled at the suggestion. "That's not a bad idea, but somehow I don't think she'd be too keen on the idea, considering the chemicals and sandpaper I'll be using. Her nails are always perfectly manicured."

"Everything about her is perfectly manicured," Roz added, then sneezed.

Sadie held back a laugh as they stopped to greet Pastor Don Sweeting, who was walking toward them on the sidewalk from Campfire Chapel into town.

"Good afternoon, ladies."

"Hi, Pastor Sweeting," Roz said.

"It's good to see you," Sadie added.

The smile lines on Don's dark skin deepened. "With the weather so perfect this morning, I decided to walk to Flap Jack's for a plate of pumpkin pancakes."

"Jeanne is out of town?" Roz asked.

Jeanne Sweeting often visited her mother in Fort Collins when she wasn't busy volunteering in Silver Peak or giving piano lessons.

"How did you guess?" the older man said with a grin, patting his stomach. "It wasn't a hard decision when I was looking at a bowl of cold cereal versus pancakes with real maple syrup and a bottomless cup of coffee. And what about the two of you?"

"I met the new owner of the Browning House yesterday, and we're on our way to take a peek inside."

"I heard someone had been willed the property," the pastor said. "I'll have to drop by as well in a day or two and welcome them to Silver Peak."

"Enjoy your day, and be sure and say hi to your wife for us when you talk to her," Sadie said, after chatting with the pastor for a couple more minutes about a new idea Julie had for the Campfire Circle Ministry that helped needy families in town.

"I certainly will."

A few minutes later, Sadie and Roz stopped on the curb in front of the large house that had been known for decades as the

Browning House. Built in the late 1800s, it was set on an oversize yard. For as long as Sadie could remember, the house had been rented out to an eclectic assortment of tenants who, in the end, had left the place run-down and in need of a large dose of TLC.

While the Browning House was smaller than some that were now being used as bed-and-breakfasts in town, it still exhibited many of the typical features of a Victorian house: patterned brown bricks, a gray slat roof with small carved ornaments where the pitched roof met, and latticework surrounding the front porch that led to the main door of the home.

Sadie remembered reading about the Browning House in one of her books about Colorado history. It gave her the background of the owners along with a number of other houses in the vicinity. Sammy Browning had arrived in Silver Peak in the late 1880s with his Indian wife and a small group of prospectors who, unlike many discouraged gold seekers who'd returned home, were still looking to strike it rich. After discovering a silver vein outside Silver Peak, Browning decided to build a house for himself and his family and settle in the Rocky Mountains.

Sadie stopped at the bottom of the stairs that led to the front porch. It had always been the history behind things that interested her as much as—if not more than—the piece itself. She took in the stone plaque marking the name and date above the front door: BROWNING HOUSE. 1887. Even after the Browning House sold to the Solomons, the name had stuck.

Starting up the stairs of the front porch, though, she paused again as she tested one of the steps with her foot. "Be careful, Roz. I have a feeling it wouldn't take much for one of these steps to cave in."

"Yikes!" Roz stopped in midstride, then gingerly maneuvered around the questionable board. "This house really does need a lot of repair."

"Which is a pity, because I can only imagine how beautiful it was at one time."

Sadie knocked on the door. Despite the general disrepair, she was quite certain that the door, with panels of stained glass to let the light in, was original to the house. If some of the original features had been saved on the inside—like Marge's bedroom set—restoring the house would definitely be worth the effort.

A minute later, Ashley opened the door wearing jeans and a Denver Broncos sweatshirt, her hair pulled back in a floppy bun and a smear of paint across her collarbone. A smile played on the edges of her lips. "Sadie, hi! Welcome."

Sadie smiled. "I hope this isn't a bad time."

"No, not at all." Ashley pushed back a strand of hair behind her ear that had fallen in front of her eye. "But you have to promise to excuse the mess. The previous renters took off in the middle of the night and left such a disaster. I'm worried it's going to take weeks just to get the place livable again."

"Please. Don't worry about it," Sadie said. "Oh, and this is my good friend, Roz Putnam. She asked if she could tag along and see the house as well."

"It's nice to meet you," Roz said. "I'm sorry to hear about your grandfather."

"Thank you, Roz. I appreciate it. And please, come on in," Ashley said, opening the door wider before stepping aside.

Sadie stopped in the middle of the entryway. She peered into the living room to the right, where a few pieces of furniture were covered with sheets. To the left a wooden staircase led to the second floor. The details inside the house were—as she'd expected—run-down, but still as stunning as she'd hoped. The original floors, the pictures carved into the wood trim, the plaster cornices and ceiling roses, and the moulded skirtings... She'd been right. With so many of the original features still in place, restoring the house would definitely be worth the expense.

"This place is beautiful," Sadie said.

"Ashley?" A man in his early forties stepped into the entryway behind Ashley and smiled. "Sorry. I didn't realize we had company."

"This is Sadie Speers, the woman I met at the estate sale, and her friend Roz," Ashley said, tugging on the hem of her sweatshirt.

"Hi, I'm Adam Solomon." The balding man held out his hand. "I'm Ashley's uncle. I had some time off and decided to come up here with her to work out the logistics of the property."

"That must be a huge help for you, Ashley."

The young woman nodded. "Oh, it definitely is. Except I keep thinking about the possibilities of this house, and my uncle's more of a realist. At least when it comes to finances."

"Part of the problem is that it's too small really to be used as a B and B," Adam said. "Yet most prospective buyers—and even renters, for that matter—want new wood flooring, granite countertops, and upgraded appliances and bathrooms."

"I still say it has potential," Ashley said. "But why don't I give you a tour, since that's what you came for, and you can decide for yourselves."

Sadie grinned at Roz. "I'd love that."

"Then if you'll excuse me," Adam said, smiling in return, "I'll go back to trying to fix the leaky bathroom sink I've been working on all morning."

Despite the neglect and an appalling lack of maintenance over the years, Sadie couldn't help but be excited. The house was the perfect blank slate for a renovation. And while restoring the home to its previous splendor wouldn't be cheap for whoever took on the project, she was thrilled to find that there were still quite a few of the original features in place. Stained glass adorned several doorways and windows, the floors comprised the typical brown terra-cotta tiles of that era, and fireplaces graced every room. Even the carpenter's work still showed the quality of the internal finishes with the elaborately carved and decorated balusters that had been carved into intricate fretwork. Workmanship that would be almost unattainable today, Sadie thought to herself. Just another reason she loved old things so much.

It didn't take much of an imagination to picture the house the way it had once looked, Sadie decided. She could almost see the addition of heavily patterned carpets with geometric motifs, floral-patterned wallpaper on the walls, and period furnishings in the rooms.

Twenty minutes later, they ended back in the living room, where Sadie had asked to save the rumored—and rare—Van Briggle fireplace for last.

"This is it." Ashley said, tugging on the bottom of her sweatshirt, a habit Sadie had picked up on, as the three of them stood in front of the fireplace. "Do you believe it's genuine?"

Sadie took her time to study the features. A hundred years ago, the jade-green tiles would have been considered more of an upgrade than a rarity. Today, though, the sought-after features could potentially add ten thousand dollars to the price of the house for the right buyer.

Sadie took a step forward and ran her fingers across one of the tiles, eager to examine them. "Van Briggle tiles have a satin sheen with slightly different hues. Like this one. But there's also the tile size to consider. True Van Briggles will be six-inch squares. Smaller rectangles are usually older Victorian tiles. So the size is right as well."

"So is it genuine?" Roz prodded.

"Yes, I believe so, based on what I can see here." Sadie took a step back and smiled. "To be a hundred percent sure, I'd want to check the back of one of the tiles. If there's a *VB* stamped on the back of one of the tiles, then I think we can be certain this is the real thing."

Roz turned to Sadie with a puzzled look. "I thought Van Briggles used the double A logo on their pieces. You know, for Artus and Anne."

Sadie nodded. "Well, yes, you're right. But on the original tiles, they were stamped with a *VB*, for Van Briggle."

"Well, it would be amazing to find another true Van Briggle fireplace. I know they're quite rare." She turned to Ashley. "And they can add substantially to a house's value."

Sadie began to respond to her friend, but paused, noting the consternation on Ashley's puckered brow.

"I guess I should be happy," Ashley began, "but to be honest, I'm not sure why my grandpa left this place to me in his will. While I'd love to restore it, there's no way I could ever afford it, and besides that, this house . . . well, to be honest, it gives me the creeps."

Sadie caught the shadow that crossed Ashley's expression. "Why is that?"

"My imagination. At least that's what my uncle says."

"What do you mean?" Roz asked.

Ashley leaned against the back of a covered piece of furniture and took in a deep breath. "Like I said, it's probably just my imagination working overtime, but I've thought more than once that someone's broken into the Browning House at night."

Sadie leaned forward. "Break-ins?"

"Not that I believe half of the stories I've heard from my uncle, but there have been a number of strange things happening. Or at least I think so."

"Like?" Sadie prodded.

"For the past few days I've been the last to leave and the first to arrive the next morning. Thankfully Adam's able to work from his hotel room, but that leaves me here alone for a few hours every day. Sometimes it's just silly things, like I had a box of granola bars I left in the house. I went to grab one this morning and half of them were gone."

"A mouse perhaps?" Roz asked.

"There are definitely mice—another thing that creeps me out." Ashley laughed, but her smile didn't last. "Some mornings when I arrive, I notice furniture has been moved, or doors I know were shut, have been opened."

"That is odd," Sadie said.

"Like I said, it's probably just my imagination, though Adam has told me stories of the Browning House ghost."

Sadie glanced at Roz. "I don't believe in ghosts, but there have been a number of odd things happening in town as well."

"What do you mean?" Ashley asked.

Roz glanced around her as if someone else might overhear. "Well, it seems that someone's been breaking into the hardware store and stealing odds and ends, like hammers and nails."

"Which makes me think we've got a thief on the loose, not a ghost." Sadie's laugh broke through the tension.

"A thief who steals hammers, nails, and granola bars," Ashley said with a shiver.

Or perhaps someone was searching for something, Sadie thought. But why the Browning House? Why Putnam & Sons?

"Have you noticed anything else missing?" Sadie asked.

"Not that I can tell," Ashley said. "Though, to be honest, I probably wouldn't notice. I'm just ready to get home and put this project behind me."

"I'm sure there's nothing to worry about," Sadie said. She glanced at her watch. "But I'll have something to worry about if I don't get back to the store soon. I'm in the middle of a refurbishing project myself, and clearly you and your uncle have your work cut out for you."

"Sadie's right. We should let you get back to work. But it was a delight to finally see this old house," Roz said, "and it was so nice to meet you."

"And you as well," Ashley said, clasping her hands together. "I appreciate your advice on the house too. I think financially my only option is to sell, but maybe the next owners will be able to restore the house."

"We can hope so," Sadie said.

"Actually, I do have one other question," Ashley said as they started toward the front door. "I wondered if you might be interested in looking through my grandpa's books. For your shop."

"I'd love to, but are you sure you want to do that? I mean, for sentimental reasons?"

"Well, I do feel sentimental toward them because of who they belonged to. But they'd just end up sitting on my bookshelf." Ashley leaned against the railing, facing Sadie and Roz. "Besides, I could tell you were intrigued. So I figured, maybe someone else can get better use out of them than I can."

"Well, Sadie has a weakness for first-edition books," Roz said, then laughed. "Or any old book for that matter, so you've asked the right person, that's for sure."

"Great," Ashley said with a smile. "The only things I want to hold on to are the photos I found inside them."

"Of course," Sadie offered. "My shop's on Main Street. Can't miss it. It's called the Antique Mine. Bring the books over whenever you're ready."

"I will. Thank you. And who knows? By the time we're finished here, there might be a few pieces of furniture you might be interested in as well."

After giving Ashley her business card and saying good-bye, Sadie and Roz headed back toward town and the Antique Mine.

"I definitely understand her hesitation in fixing up that house, but wow, wouldn't it be stunning with some restoration?" Sadie said.

"That's for sure." Roz's phone rang and she pulled it out of the pocket of her colorful patchwork jacket. "It's Roscoe."

A minute later Roz hung up the call. "You're not going to believe this."

"More muddy footprints at Putnam & Sons?" Sadie teased.

Roz stopped in the middle of the sidewalk and shook her head. "No, this might be even stranger than the footprints."

"Meaning?" Sadie prodded.

"Roscoe just opened up the shop. Apparently someone broke in again during the night. And this time, they stole Roscoe's chess set."

5

At six o'clock that evening, Sadie parked outside her daughter's 1940s-style home after working at the Antique Mine all day. She'd managed to make considerable progress on Marge's furniture, despite the distressing news of yet another theft at the hardware store. Sadie couldn't stop her mind from turning over the lingering question of who might be breaking in—both at the hardware store *and* at the Browning House. And why steal a chess set, of all things?

She turned the car off and made her way to Alice's front door. Alice smiled as she opened the door.

"Something smells delicious," Sadie said, stepping into the cozy home.

"Lasagna from the Market, and"—Alice shot her mother a grin—"a surprise."

Her interest piqued, Sadie followed her daughter toward the kitchen. Both taller and slimmer than Sadie, Alice had auburn hair and green eyes that were legacies from her father.

Sadie stepped into the kitchen and breathed in the aroma of fruit, sugar, and cinnamon. "What's the surprise?"

"Raspberries." Alice pointed to four plastic buckets of fruit sitting beside her on the counter. "And in the oven there's a raspberry pie."

"Yum. Where in the world did you get so many this time of year?"

"The mom of one of my students wanted to thank me for helping her son with some extra tutoring." Alice, who taught at the local Silver Peak elementary school, was always bringing home gifts from her students. "Which means I've got raspberries from her berry patch coming out of my ears. Not that I'm complaining, mind you!" Alice leaned against the counter where she'd been snapping a bowl of green beans. "Theo's asking for ice cream, and Sara wants me to make jam. I'll probably end up freezing most of them and pulling them out for muffins and banana bread over the winter. For this pie, I dug out Grandma Wright's recipe and threw it together after school."

"I'm impressed." Cooking from scratch wasn't something Alice normally had time for, especially during the school year. "I'll never forget berry-picking in the summers, along with my mom's pies."

"I remember wearing jeans, sweaters, and tennis shoes—even in the summertime—in order to brave the thorns. And it was entirely worth it!"

"I remember how you usually ended up back home with your bucket barely halfway full."

"I still love them." Alice laughed, then pointed to the green beans. "Do you mind putting together the salad while I finish snapping these?"

"Not at all. Another gift from your students' parents?" Sadie asked as she started chopping up a tomato that sat on the cutting board.

"These actually came from Harry. His beans did exceptionally well this year, and you know Harry, always giving things away."

Harry Polmiller never ceased to amaze Sadie. At ninety-four, he was still active and had one of the largest vegetable gardens in town. With its dry climate and short growing season, Silver Peak was not the easiest place to grow a garden. Yet Harry made it seem simple.

Sadie finished chopping up the tomato, then drew in a deep breath as Alice pulled the dessert out of the oven. "I don't know about you, but I'd be content to skip dinner and go straight to that raspberry pie. It smells incredible."

With the pie set on the counter to cool, Alice then dumped the beans into a colander and started rinsing them in the sink. "I've been thinking about you and that new refurbishing project you told me about on the phone."

"Don't tell me you're going to start nagging me over taking on too big of a project?"

"Like everyone else in town, I know Marge." Alice glanced at Sadie. "Did she come by again today?"

"Yes." Sadie dumped the chopped tomato into the bowl, then reached for a cucumber. "I'll admit that while the woman's always been somewhat of a thorn in my side, she's being extrademanding right now."

"How so?"

"Well, her sister and brother-in-law are flying in at the end of next week with her mother, and she wants me to be finished before they arrive."

"Hey, Grandma." Sara, Alice's fourteen-year-old daughter, slipped into the kitchen and grabbed a few raspberries out of one of the buckets, interrupting their conversation. That was fine with Sadie. It made her blood pressure escalate a little just thinking about Marge's news this morning.

"We're not going to have any left if you keep sneaking in here, young lady." Alice nudged her daughter with her elbow, clearly amused.

Sara grinned across the kitchen at Sadie, then started out the back door, her strawberry-blonde ponytail swinging behind her. "I can't help it. They're so good."

"I have to agree with you there." Alice dumped the green beans into a pot of water that had just come to a boil on the stove. "But where are you going, Sara? Dinner's about ready."

"I just need five minutes to check on Millie." Sara shot her mom an imploring look. "Please?"

Alice hesitated. "Five minutes. Dinner's almost ready, and it will get cold if we wait too long."

"Who's Millie?" Sadie asked. Knowing Sara, it was another animal she'd managed to rescue.

"You know Sara." Alice rolled her eyes. "A stray kitten she found last night. It's sleeping out in a box on the back porch with a blanket. We're still trying to find out who it belongs to. Dr. Armstead stopped by last night. You know how he's always been so good to give Sara advice and free care."

True to her word, Sara bounced back into the house on time, and the four of them sat down at the kitchen table while Theo, Sadie's grandson, prayed a blessing over the food before they all dug in.

"Grandma," Theo said, helping himself to a slice of toasted garlic bread, before passing the plate on to his mother. "I heard something strange has been going on at Roscoe's shop. What's up?"

"What makes you think I'd know?" Sadie said with a grin. She sprinkled some shredded Parmesan cheese onto her lasagna. "Someone's been breaking into the shop, apparently on a regular basis, and stealing odds and ends."

"That's weird," Theo said.

"Especially since the items that have been stolen aren't worth all that much," Sadie said.

Theo pushed a lock of dark hair out of his eyes, then passed the bread to his sister. "Does Mr. Putnam have any idea who it is?"

"Last I heard, the sheriff hasn't been able to come up with any leads. The strangest part is, there are no physical signs of a break-in. The only real evidence, besides the missing inventory, is some muddy footprints that were left yesterday morning inside the store."

"Sounds like someone has a key and can let themselves in," Sara said.

"That's my guess," Sadie agreed. "But only because it's the one thing that makes sense. And like I said, so far they've just taken small stuff. Until this morning."

Theo leaned forward, clearly intrigued by the mystery. "What did they steal this morning?"

"The antique chess set Roz got Roscoe for his birthday."

"A chess set?" Alice asked.

"Strange, isn't it? Roscoe had the idea of setting it up in the corner of the shop for his customers to play with while they shoot the breeze. Such a piece of Americana. Then this morning, when he went to open up the shop, it was gone."

"What's the chess set worth?" Theo drizzled dressing on his salad.

"I was reading a magazine at Doc Conroy's office a while back and saw a photo of a chess set worth over half a million dollars," Alice commented.

"Half a million dollars?" Sara's eyes widened. "What was it made out of, diamonds?"

"Actually, yes. Over four pounds of gold and studded with black and white diamonds."

Theo let out a low whistle. "That's crazy."

"Well, Roscoe's chess set was handmade and beautifully carved, but trust me, no gold or diamonds."

"But if the board isn't worth much, why steal it?" Alice asked.

Sara leaned forward, holding up her fork for emphasis. "Maybe it holds some sort of secret."

"Ooh, good idea," Theo said. "What did the board look like?"

"It was made of cherrywood, with some leather finishings on the side and a drawer to store the pieces underneath." Sadie glanced at the garlic bread in front of her, then decided she'd better skip a second piece in order to save room for raspberry pie. "And actually, now that you mention it, there were some interesting markings on the board itself that were carved along the upper sides of the wood."

Clearly Sadie's observations had piqued Theo's and Sara's interest. "What kind of markings?"

"They looked something like cursive letters, but I am assuming they were just meant for decoration."

"What other things were stolen from the shop?" Alice asked.

"Before today, just things like flashlights. Batteries. Nails and a hammer. Perhaps a few other odds and ends. Roscoe's just finished a full inventory for Mac."

"What about the footprints?" Theo asked. "Could you tell where they were coming from?"

"I can do better than that. I can show you." Sadie grabbed her purse from the back of her chair and pulled out her phone. "Roscoe sent me the photos he took of them. Take a look at them before I tell you what I think."

Theo zoomed in on one of the photos, studied it a moment, then passed the phone to his mom, who in turn passed it to Sara.

"Notice anything interesting?" Sadie asked.

"It almost looks as if there are another set of prints that someone tried to wipe away," Theo said.

"That's exactly what I thought," Sadie said.

"But why?"

Sadie looked to Alice. "Apparently there have been a string of break-ins in several of the nearby towns."

"I heard about those on the news," Theo said. "And the sheriff thinks this is connected?"

"It's a theory." Sadie smiled. With his skills in critical thinking, her grandson would make a great detective someday.

"What about your shop, Mom?"

Sadie caught the worry in her daughter's eyes. "I haven't noticed anything out of place or missing."

"I have an idea. How about we do a stakeout?" Theo glanced up at Sadie, then raised his eyebrows.

"A stakeout?" Sadie wanted to laugh at the absurdity of the mental picture the word formed in her mind, but Theo clearly was serious. Alice and Sara leaned in with apparent curiosity.

"You know. Every crime novel has one in it. Late-night stakeouts with a bunch of coffee and a long-lens camera." He laughed. "You know, I've always wanted to do something like that."

"I love that idea in theory," Sadie said, "but an all-nighter isn't exactly my cup of tea these days." Theo shrugged. But it got Sadie thinking. While the traditional stakeout might not be the answer, Theo was right about one thing. They needed to catch the thief in the act. She just wasn't sure how.

As soon as they'd finished the meal, Sara scooted her chair back. "I don't know about the rest of you, but I'm ready for dessert."

"So am I," Alice agreed. "Theo... Sara... if the two of you will clear and rinse the dishes, I'll serve up the pie."

Sadie got up to help her grandchildren by grabbing the half-empty dish of lasagna and carrying it into the kitchen.

"Okay, then how about another idea?" Theo said, clearly not ready to give up. "We could put a camera inside the hardware shop."

"You mean install a surveillance system?" Sadie asked.

"Exactly."

The idea was a good one, but Sadie wasn't sure whether Roscoe would go for it. "I might be wrong, but I suspect Roscoe would say forget it. He's more frugal than I am, and when I looked into putting in a surveillance system a few years ago, it cost far more than I wanted to shell out."

The sleepy town of Silver Peak had rarely been a place where people ever needed to worry about surveillance systems.

"If you hire a company to install it, you're right," Theo said, handing a rinsed plate to Sara to put in the dishwasher. "It *is* expensive, but you don't have to do it through a company."

"What do you mean?" Sadie asked. "You could do it yourself?"

"Why not?" Theo turned off the water, then wiped his hands on a dish towel. "You can turn the webcam on your computer into a video surveillance camera monitor with your phone or laptop. Download some software for free, and it should be simple to install and cost practically nothing."

"Could you help Roscoe set it up?" Sadie asked.

"Sure. He'd be able to see everything that's going on at night."

Roscoe would probably go for that. "It's up to Roscoe, of course, since it is his shop."

"Cool. I can help him by getting the equipment if he wants."

"Do you think you could really find out what's going on that way?" Alice asked.

"I suppose there's no way to know unless we try," Sadie said.

"What about your test, Theo?" Alice asked.

"I'm ready for it."

"Well then, I don't have a problem with your going."

"Let me give Roscoe a call," Sadie said. "As soon as we're done with the pie, we can see if he'll meet us at the store."

Sadie and Roz looked on as Theo began setting up a computer and small Web camera at Putnam & Sons for an improvised surveillance system.

"Are you sure this is going to work?" Roscoe asked.

"I don't see why not. The minute your thief walks through that door, he should be caught on camera."

Sadie watched her grandson work, impressed with his skills. While she had her own smartphone and considered herself fairly up-to-date with technology, this was definitely beyond her skill level.

"It's just a basic system," Theo explained. "We won't be able to view a live stream of video, but when the app detects motion it will start recording, and then we'll be able to watch that."

"Like when our thief shows up."

"Exactly," Theo said. "Any motion will start the recording. I'm downloading and installing the app on this cell phone and setting up an account. I'll give the app permission to access our device and use it as a video camera, which will turn on the motion-detection feature. We won't be able to get an entire one-hundred-and-eighty-degree shot, but that shouldn't matter. We've got the front door covered, as well as the cash register."

"So what do we do now?" Roz asked.

"We wait," Sadie said with a smile. "And then we catch ourselves a thief."

6

On Saturday morning, Sadie slipped into the back room of the Antique Mine, eager to begin working on Marge's dresser and headboard. She'd already finished the tedious process of sanding the furniture with progressively finer grains of sandpaper in order to get rid of any loose wood fibers. Today, she was applying the second coat of shellac. Pressing the pad of cotton and shellac she'd prepared on the back of her hand, she continued to gently sweep it across the headboard, leaving a thin layer of the shellac on the surface. After repeating this process six or seven times and allowing each layer to dry in between, she'd eventually achieve the glossy, mirrorlike finish she was after.

She'd first learned this polishing process from her French friend, Jean-Pierre, who'd become a wonderful source of information on both antiques and refurbishing techniques. And while most manufacturers had abandoned the labor-intensive technique in the 1930s, opting instead for a spray finish or abrasive buffing, Sadie enjoyed trying different techniques. This technique in particular worked especially well with mahogany and other expensive woods, as it gave the furniture a high-gloss surface with deep color.

Sadie hummed along with George Jones as "He Stopped Loving Her Today" played over the speakers in her store. The tear-jerking song was one of her old favorites, and she felt the muscles in her neck begin to relax as she continued her work. Her mind turned over the strange things that had been happening next door. When she'd spoken briefly to Theo earlier, he had already checked the video footage, but Roscoe's mysterious visitor had failed to make an appearance the night before. Theo promised Roscoe that he would reset it again for tonight and keep checking until they got something. And while it might be a long shot, it seemed like their best bet at the moment.

She'd just finished the second layer when the bell over the front door jingled, signaling Julie's arrival.

"Sadie?" she called.

"I'm back here."

A moment later, Julie stepped into the back room wearing jeans and a purple sweater. While Sadie's assistant had a love for vintage clothing, today she had chosen something simpler and more casual.

"Morning, Sadie." Julie put her sack lunch into the small refrigerator Sadie had bought for her employees.

"How is Brody's cough?" Sadie asked.

"Much better. I actually got a good night's sleep." One of Julie's ten-year-old twins had come down with a bad cold over the weekend and was still struggling to get rid of it. "Of course, it also helps to have a pediatrician as a husband."

"I bet." Sadie laughed. "Which is why, with all that's going on, I appreciate your coming in today. I know you've worked quite a few hours the past few weeks."

Julie's smile broadened. "You know how much I love working here. It gives me something to do that I enjoy. What are your plans for the day?"

"If you wouldn't mind opening the store this morning, I need to finish this layer. Then, later, Roz and I are planning to visit James Abbott."

"Are you going to another estate sale?"

"Not this time." Sadie continued her work, carefully moving in the direction of the wood grain across the headboard. "Actually, we need to speak to him about the chess set Roz bought Roscoe for his birthday. It's probably a long shot, but we're hoping he might know something that could point to why someone would want to steal it."

Julie set her purse down on the small table and frowned. "I heard about that."

"Roscoe discovered it was missing yesterday when he went in to work." Sadie looked up. "Which reminds me. You haven't noticed anything missing from our shop, have you?"

"No. Has the hardware ghost hit any other stores?" Julie teased.

"Not as far as I know," Sadie said with a grin. "But until they find out who's behind this, the sheriff wants us to watch for anything that seems off."

"Of course." Julie's smile faded. "Because as silly as it sounds to talk about a ghost in the hardware store, the idea of a thief on the loose in Silver Peak is pretty unsettling."

An hour later, Sadie and Roz pulled into the parking lot of the company that had handled the estate sale of Danny Solomon.

Sadie was thankful Roz had decided to join her since it was her chess set that had been stolen. And Julie had been right. While the idea of a ghost breaking into Putnam & Sons was silly, the thought that a group of thieves could be hitting their town wasn't funny at all. And while their visit here might turn out to be fruitless, she hoped something James might say could give her a clue as to why someone would want to steal Roscoe's chess set.

Sadie had worked with the estate manager on numerous occasions over the past ten years. The older man organized many of the local estate sales she attended, from Colorado Springs to Arvada, as he helped liquidate the majority of household items in particular after a family member passed away. While Sadie had heard stories of similar services that took advantage of their clients, she'd always found James's prices to be fair, and she had appreciated the way he dealt with the families—especially during times of loss—as both professional and compassionate.

Because his office was located thirty minutes outside of Silver Peak in a nearby town, Sadie had debated with Roz whether they should simply make a phone call rather than chat in person. But if she and Roz were going to discover what was going on at Putnam & Sons, the most logical thing in her mind was to start with the chess set itself. Sadie knew from experience that a face-to-face conversation could often reveal things that a phone call could keep hidden. Which meant meeting with James in person in order to find out more about the family and the chess set Roz had bought made sense.

"Do you think we're just grasping at straws?" Roz asked as she took off her seat belt.

"Possibly, but at least I feel like we're doing something. It might be just an inexpensive chess set we're looking into, but it feels funny to ask about some missing generic screwdrivers and bolts. At least this is a place to start."

Roz laughed. "You definitely have a point."

Sadie glanced at her watch as she followed Roz up the sidewalk toward the building. Its large windows reflected the grandeur of the mountains in the distance. When she'd called James, he'd assured her that he would be in the office this morning. And true to his word, James met them at the front door of the reception area.

"Morning, Sadie. Hi, Roz. It's good to see both of you again." James rested his hands against his ample midsection. "After your mysterious phone call, I deduced you're trying to get a sneak peek at our next sale. Am I right?"

"I...," Sadie started to explain, but James didn't give her a chance to continue.

"Because I actually have a client who needs to raise some capital for a new venture. He has quite a collection of paintings by local artists he's decided to let go of, along with a handful of other valuable antiques. Now *that's* a sale you won't want to miss."

"You know Sadie too well," Roz said with a laugh.

"You're both right," Sadie said. "And I'll definitely plan to be there. I have a dozen clients I could name off the top of my head who are always interested in art, but especially if it is done by someone locally."

"Just as I thought. I'll be sure to have my assistant send you all of the details of the sale"—he leaned forward before adding in conspiratorial tones—"including the private showing we're planning to do the day before that will include a few handpicked buyers like yourself."

Sadie smiled at his clandestine manner. "I'm already looking forward to it. And I appreciate your letting us drop by," Sadie said. "Actually, though, Roz and I are here hoping you can help us with some information about the last sale we attended."

James motioned them into his office adjacent to the front room, then offered them the two empty chairs in front of his desk. "I saw you snatch up that bedroom set without any hesitation. You clearly have an eye for quality, Sadie. Most people I spoke with that day told me it would be far too time-consuming to try to restore it."

Sadie chuckled. "I've been reminded of that fact a number of times, but while I'm sure it will be a lot of work, I have to say I'm enjoying the process so far. The finished piece is going to be stunning and worth far more than what I paid for it."

"And that chess set you picked up, Roz." James leaned back in his chair. "I thought about buying it myself, but if I did that at every sale I organized, I'd be forced to have my own liquidation sale."

Roz laughed. "Well, since you mentioned it, it's the chess set we need to talk to you about."

James's gaze narrowed. "I hope you weren't thinking of returning it. Unfortunately all sales are final. Management's rules."

Roz glanced at Sadie, then back to James. "Oh, certainly not. It's gorgeous. I gave it to my husband on his birthday a few days ago, and he loves it."

"Then I'm not sure I understand." James's fingers drummed against the desk. "Is there a problem with the chess set?"

"Not a problem, per se. At least not with the chess set itself." Sadie hesitated. "But it was stolen last night from Roz's husband's hardware store in Silver Peak."

"Stolen?" James stopped drumming and sat back in his chair. "That is strange. Granted, it was a beautiful piece and hand-carved, from what I understand, by the deceased's grandfather, but it wasn't worth a lot monetarily. Now, there are some particular artists that collectors seek, and those chess sets can go for a pretty penny. Louis Solomon was a good craftsman, don't get me wrong, but he wasn't in that league."

"Which is what we're trying to understand," Roz said. "Why would someone want to steal it?"

"I don't know." James slid off his glasses and rubbed his eyes before continuing. "You've heard about the ring of thieves that's been hitting around here locally?"

Roz shot a glance at Sadie. "Yes."

"Maybe they've decided to hit Silver Peak."

"I thought about that too. And Mac Slattery, our sheriff, is considering that option," Sadie said. "But you have to admit that the chess set is an odd piece to steal, even if it is the same ring of thieves."

Sadie thought of the other odds and ends that had been stolen from Roscoe's shop, and figured those, too, weren't valuable enough to interest professional thieves. And then, of course, there were the strange things Ashley had told them about at the Browning House. Somewhere, she couldn't help thinking, there was a connection. But what?

"You have a point." The man scratched the back of his head. "Though it would seem you aren't the only one who wants to get their hands on it. Someone called me not thirty minutes ago asking about the piece."

"Really?" Sadie leaned forward. "What did they want?"

"The chess set itself. Ashley King, Danny Solomon's granddaughter, claimed that the chess set was given to her in the will by her grandfather."

Sadie looked at Roz. Could Ashley, believing that the chess set should have gone to her, have stolen it from the hardware store? Sadie frowned at the thought. Whoever had been breaking into Putnam & Sons had been doing so for weeks. Ashley and her uncle had just arrived. On the other hand, Ashley clearly did have motivation. But why would she call asking for information if she already had the piece?

"I don't know." James dropped his pen onto his desk, interrupting Sadie's thoughts. "She seems like such a nice young woman."

"What exactly did Ashley say on the telephone?" Sadie asked.

"She said she had just received information from the family lawyer that her grandfather left her the chess set." James was back to drumming his pen against his desk. "I've just put in a call to see if I can find out what happened, but I've already rechecked the paperwork I have. All I know is that she was left a box full of rare edition books and..."

"A house in Silver Peak," Sadie said.

James's thick brows rose. "How do you know about the house?"

"Roz and I visited her and her uncle yesterday. Unfortunately the house needs a lot of restoration, which requires capital she doesn't have. And she's worried it won't be easy to sell."

"Makes you wonder why the old man left it to her," James said, shaking his head.

"That was her question," Roz said. "But you're sure about the chess set? I'd feel terrible if I had bought part of her inheritance."

"It wouldn't be the first time we've discovered a mix-up. Like I said, I left a message for the lawyer right before you arrived to see if he knows anything, but to be honest…I wouldn't worry about it, Roz. These estate sales are always difficult for the family. And they can be contentious when an heir finds out they didn't get something they wanted or had been promised." He seemed to think for a moment. "Of course, knowing the item was stolen does make me wonder what else is going on."

"Should we go talk to her again?" Roz asked Sadie. "And let her know what happened? I really do feel terrible."

"I wouldn't," James said. "My advice would be to hold off even mentioning the chess set for the time being. Give me a few days to sort things out with the executor of the will and, in the meantime, maybe the chess set will show up on its own."

"You're probably right," Sadie said, nodding in agreement. "One more question. Do you know anything about Danny Solomon?"

"Danny Solomon? Now there's a character for you."

"You knew him?" Sadie asked. While learning too much more of the chess set's history seemed unlikely at this point, any information she could gather couldn't hurt.

"I never met the man, but after his family left Silver Peak a few decades ago, they settled down in Walsenburg. I heard rumors for years that he and his family were involved in some shady things, going all the way back to Prohibition and later with the Mountain Mafia."

"I thought the Mountain Mafia wasn't active anymore," Roz said.

"Just because they dissolved doesn't mean those involved cleaned up their acts, or their reputations. I'll leave it up to you as to how much of the rumors you believe."

With that, Sadie and Roz stood and thanked James for his time, then headed for the car. Sadie breathed in a lungful of the cool mountain air, another reminder that winter was on its way. But she still didn't feel any closer to the truth. In fact, her visit to James had only managed to raise more questions. If Ashley really believed the chess set was hers, would that be enough motivation for her to break in to a store and steal it?

7

SADIE'S FINGERS GRIPPED THE STEERING WHEEL AS SHE DROVE with Roz along Route 65 toward Silver Peak from the estate agent's office. Growing up, her parents had enjoyed teaching her new things and had made travel a priority—as much as their budget had allowed. That was partly where she'd got her interest in history and antiques. But while she still loved to travel and visit new places, there was nothing more calming to her soul than driving through the mountains when the Colorado foothills were blanketed with the shimmering yellows and golds of aspen trees. And it was the perfect setting to let her mind work.

Like today, when none of the pieces of the puzzle seemed to fit.

She mulled through the information James had just given them. Somehow, she just couldn't see Ashley breaking into the hardware store simply to steal a chess set. It didn't make sense. Especially knowing she'd called—after the theft—to ask about it. Something didn't add up.

"So what do you think, Roz?" Sadie broke the companionable silence they'd enjoyed for several miles as they followed the winding, narrow road.

"About the thefts? Or about the odd goings-on at Roscoe's store?" Roz tapped the armrest and frowned. "At this point, all I know for sure is that I bought a chess set that Ashley King believes is hers. And I don't think it has anything to do with the break-ins."

Sadie nodded. "I don't think so either."

Roz was silent for a moment more, then added, "And I wouldn't blame Ashley if she wanted the chess set, knowing her great-great-grandfather had hand-carved it."

"I know I would want it if I were her."

With no real answers, the two of them fell back into a thoughtful silence.

Thirty minutes later, Sadie drove down Main Street, pulled into a space in front of the Antique Mine, then frowned at Marge's car parked in front of them. "Do you see what I see?"

Roz nodded and flashed her an *I-told-you-so* grin. "Yep."

"I've only been working on the bedroom a couple of days, and she's already stopped by every day so far."

"I hate to leave you to deal with Marge on your own, but I promised I'd meet Roscoe as soon as we got back."

"No worries, Roz. I'll see you later."

Marge stood at the counter chatting with Julie when Sadie walked into the store.

"Morning, Sadie," Marge said, her voice colder than normal. "I had to stop by the Market for some groceries and thought I'd drop in and see how things are going. Julie let me take a peek at your progress."

Sadie frowned. Clearly Marge was unhappy with what she'd seen.

The front bell jingled as two older women walked in, chatting.

Julie shot Sadie a look of apology and shrugged, then went to help the new customers.

"Good morning, Marge." Sadie stopped at the counter next to Marge. "I've finished all of the sanding and have already applied two layers of the shellac. I'm letting the second layer dry now."

The woman's frown deepened, her nails tapping against the countertop. "I assumed you'd be a little...further along in the process by now."

Further along? Sadie bit her lip before forcing a smile.

"And the color...," Marge continued. "I'm not sure about the color. I brought a sample of the wallpaper I want to use, but unfortunately, I'm not sure it's going to work now."

Marge dug the sample out of her large handbag and held it up. Pale blue background with large pink and ivory flowers with flecks of gold. The pattern was bold. Just like Marge.

"What do you think?" Marge asked, still frowning.

Sadie hesitated. Did Marge really want to know what she was thinking? Or was her mind already made up? While her own bedroom featured antiques and even a fireplace, which she especially was thankful for in the wintertime, the wallpaper pattern was too loud for her simpler tastes. But she had to concede that, for Marge, it seemed perfect.

"I think it could work," Sadie said, keeping her tone neutral. "We discussed keeping the set the natural color of the wood, though once I'm finished it will darken some..."

"I know what we discussed, but your reputation is at stake here." Marge's voice rose to a high pitch, her voice carrying across the store. "And you call yourself an antiques expert! I trusted you with this furniture, and now I don't see how I'll possibly have it when I need it most. I would think as a business owner, your customers would be your highest priority." Marge's cheeks flushed as she took a step back and gave Sadie a look that felt like the drop of a gauntlet. "Or am I wrong?"

Sadie glanced across the room to where Julie was helping two older women. All three of them stared back, mouths agape. She started to respond, then paused. Marge had always been brash, but to cause a scene like this, and in front of her customers and staff...

Sadie sucked in a shallow breath. When she spoke, she tried to keep her voice low, but it was difficult. "Marge, I told you I'd do everything I could to finish in time, but your new schedule has made that nearly impossible. You're right that my reputation is on the line here. If I cut corners and speed up the process, these pieces will be ruined, along with my reputation. You trusted me to do an expert job on this set, and I will, if you'll just give me a chance. There are things in the process that I simply can't speed up. The shellac must dry or it'll ruin the final shine. And you knew that, going in."

Sadie took a step back, immediately regretting the sharpness she'd heard creeping into her tone. As she studied Marge's wide eyes and the tension in her face, it dawned on her. Marge's outburst had nothing to do with a piece of bedroom furniture. Something else was clearly going on.

But what?

"Marge?" Sadie cleared her throat quietly. "Is there something else?"

"No."

She felt her jaw drop as Marge turned and marched out the front door, the bell jingling as it slammed shut.

Sadie was still mulling over her encounter with Marge when she cleared her dinner dishes that evening. She put them in the dishwasher, then wiped down the granite countertops. T.R. had remodeled the kitchen only a year before his death. He and Sadie had become the fourth generation to live in her family's house, and the remodeling they'd done had managed to keep the charm of the older farmhouse alongside the conveniences of twenty-first-century living.

She finished wiping the table, then put away the sponge. With its large chef's oven, stainless steel appliances, and dark cherry cupboards that reached all the way to the ceiling, the kitchen had always seemed to Sadie like something that belonged in a showroom. Or even on TV. It made her feel like a much shorter version of Julia Child—as if she could cook anything there.

But her favorite spot in the kitchen was the original antique leaded-glass window over the sink, which T.R. had lovingly restored for her, adding scrolled cherrywood trim that made it a showpiece.

Sadie looked out the window now, taking in the grandeur of her golden tree-lined view as the late afternoon sunlight filtered into the kitchen. This house held so many memories. She'd grown up here, then moved here as a new bride. Her daughter had been raised here, and her grandchildren had played in the yard, chasing each other around the towering fir trees in the summer and building snowmen in the winter.

She sighed. Try as she might, she couldn't shake her irritation after Marge's visit. The woman had always been testy, but she'd never actually yelled at Sadie before. And to have done so in front of Julie and her customers…Despite Marge's blustery and imperious manner, it was not normal for her.

But that wasn't the only thing nagging at her. Sadie knew that her own reaction hadn't exactly been commendable either.

Leaving the kitchen, Sadie stepped into the main room of the farmhouse, hoping a good book might pull her out of her sour mood. The large room was expansive with its vaulted ceilings and a beautiful, tall stone fireplace. There were built-in bookcases surrounding the fireplace, where she mainly featured books on the history of Colorado, and even more specifically, Silver Peak. She'd decorated the room in a warm, cozy Colorado style with two deep, leather lounge chairs and a couch in paisley upholstery. The coffee table—with its rustic surface—had been custom-made by her friend and local artist Josh Ralston. But Sadie wasn't focused on any of the familiar fixtures of her house at the moment. Hank came up and nudged her leg.

She bent down to rub the dog behind the ears. "I've been spending too many hours at work, haven't I? Give me a minute, and we'll go for our evening walk."

She picked up her cell phone and touched the screen to dial a familiar number.

"To what do I owe this great honor?" Edwin's deep voice sounded resonant and cheerful in her ear.

It felt good to laugh. "No reason, other than I needed to hear your voice."

"Oh? Something on your mind?"

"Well, yes. But I don't know if I'm ready to talk about it just yet. Don't worry," she hastened to add, "it has nothing to do with you."

"*Hmm*. That sounds cryptic. But you know you can always talk to me about anything."

"Yes, I know." And she did. Once again she found herself thanking God for bringing this man back into her life. "And maybe I will, later. Right now, I'm afraid I might say some very unchristian things, and I don't want to do that."

"Probably wise, then."

"I'm about to take Hank out for a *W-A-L-K*," she said, her voice dropping to a whisper as she spelled the word. "That should give me time to pray about it."

"Call me later."

They finished their call, and Sadie headed out of the back of the house with Hank in tow. Evenings were one of her favorite parts of the day, and a walk was exactly what she needed tonight. Walks along the trails with Hank allowed her to clear her mind, pray, and gain perspective on things weighing heavy on her mind. Because not only was there the situation with Marge, but there were also the strange things that had happened at Putnam & Sons. This morning, she'd spent longer than normal during her quiet time, reading through her Bible and praying. One of the verses she'd read in particular continued to replay in her mind as she started up the trail behind her house.

He revealeth the deep and secret things:
he knoweth what is in the darkness,
and the light dwelleth with him.

She took in a deep breath and let the crisp mountain air fill her lungs, feeling some of the tension that had started to take hold in the back of her neck begin to release. While Marge was the last person she felt like thinking about, she knew she had to find a way to get past her anger toward the woman. Digging beneath Marge's prickly exterior was not going to be easy, but it was something she knew she needed to do.

But how?

I just don't have a clue how to connect with her, Lord.

And if she was honest, she wasn't even sure she wanted to try. Quite frankly, she was angry with Marge. Maybe all she really could do was to keep praying that God would reveal the truth behind Marge's hurt with His light. And that she could somehow learn how to be a friend to the woman in the process. Because there was one thing she was quite certain of. She might not know exactly what it was, but she was still convinced that Marge's outburst had little to do with the bedroom set.

And her anger toward Marge might not stem only from their confrontation at the store. Sadie had always brushed off Marge's brusqueness and high-handed manner. They attended church together, after all, and Sadie tried to live by Romans 12:18: "If it is possible, as far as it depends on you, live at peace with everyone." But Marge didn't make it easy. Could the slights, snubs, and veiled insults she'd felt from Marge somehow have added up over the years? She hoped not.

Hank ran off the trail, started sniffing, then barked. Sadie caught up to him a moment later.

"What'd you find, Hank?'

She scratched the top of his head, stopping to look at whatever had caught his attention. There was a mound of dirt on the edge of the trail.

"It was one of those pocket gophers, but by the looks of that hole, he's long gone," she told him.

Hank looked up at her as if disappointed. Sadie laughed as he turned around and then bounded up the trail in front of her, his attention already latched on to something else. She kept walking, comfortable with her slower pace this evening, and she felt herself finally beginning to relax. But as much as she didn't like the idea, she knew that today wasn't going to be the last time she was going to have to deal with Marge. And finding a way to finish the restoration project and help Marge meet her deadline might end up being more difficult than discovering who'd been breaking into Putnam & Sons.

8

The next morning, Pastor Sweeting's sermon managed to hit close to home for Sadie. Today's lesson had come from Colossians 3, which spoke about the importance of making allowances for each other's faults—and forgiving the person who offended you.

And, boy, had she been offended.

But as she'd thought yesterday, whatever was going on with Marge had to run far deeper than a bedroom set she wasn't happy with. But she had no idea what the issue actually was. Or how to find out.

Sadie glanced across the church at the congregation gathered in the old clapboard sanctuary. Roz and Roscoe sat nearby. Josh Ralston was near the back. Alice and the kids were in the row with her and Edwin. There was Harry Polmiller, the oldest member, and Dr. Ben Armstead, the town veterinarian. Spike Harris, standing to one side of the platform, was waiting for the closing music to begin.

And, of course, there sat Marge Ruxton, right up near the front with her husband, Lanford.

Sadie let out a soft sigh. She might believe she was in the right when it came to the situation with Marge, but she also realized she hadn't wanted to make allowances for the woman's behavior. She knew she needed to find a way to extend grace, make allowances, and forgive the woman as today's lesson had emphasized. While she and Marge might never become best friends, she was still the one who needed to make an effort.

As soon as they finished the closing song, Pastor Sweeting dismissed the congregation with a prayer.

Sadie watched as Marge and Lanford exited their pew and headed straight for the door. Before they left, Marge turned around and locked eyes with Sadie for a fleeting moment. Could she have seen a hint of regret in Marge's expression? Or was that just wishful thinking on Sadie's part?

"Are you still up for lunch?" Edwin asked, slipping his hymnal into the slot in front of him.

Sadie shook off the discomfort of the previous moment. "Absolutely," Sadie said, realizing how hungry she was. "I'm starving."

They said good-bye to a few friends, then walked to the car together. When they were both settled and he'd started the car, he asked, "How about Los Pollitos today? Alice told me they have a new special on the menu that's supposed to be fantastic."

"Sounds good to me."

Edwin drove the short distance to the restaurant, parked along the street, then escorted Sadie inside.

The hostess seated them a few minutes later inside the cozy dining room of Los Pollitos, which was artfully decorated with a terra-cotta tile floor. In warmer weather, Sadie enjoyed sitting on the quiet, outdoor patio, but the wind was too chilly today to sit outside.

Edwin took a sip of his water. "What did you think about the sermon?" he asked.

"I always appreciate how much thought Don puts into the things he shares with the congregation, and today was no exception," Sadie said. "It hit just a touch close to home for me," she admitted, taking her own sip of water. "I realized I'm not always as patient and forgiving as I'd like to be. Especially when people rub me the wrong way."

Edwin cocked a silver eyebrow. "Anyone in particular? Does this have something to do with our cryptic conversation last night?"

Sadie nodded. Was she ready to talk it over with him? "Well..." She lowered her voice. "As you know, Marge has been coming in to the shop every day, very concerned about my newest project for her. Not only has she moved up the deadline for when she needs the furniture done, she made it quite known to me—and everyone in the store—that she's extremely unhappy with me and my work. She really threw my reputation, and me, under the bus, so to speak. And in front of other customers."

"Ouch." Edwin let out a low whistle.

"Yes. Ouch. And if that isn't bad enough, I spoke back to her pretty bluntly and sharply myself. And that bothers me as much as what she said, or how she said it."

Edwin said nothing as he waited for her to speak again. "And I've let her get under my skin all week, but just because she's not the easiest client to deal with, that doesn't mean she doesn't deserve God's grace. And my grace," she added. "But instead, I snapped right back at her."

Edwin took her hands and squeezed them, waiting for her to continue.

"The thing is," Sadie continued, "I'm sure this isn't just about a bedroom set, though I don't know what's wrong. Because she's so insistent the house is finished before her family arrives, part of me wonders if it doesn't have something to do with her family members, though I have no idea what the problems there might be. Any advice?" Sadie asked, catching Edwin's gaze.

"That's a tough one. It's not always easy to sweeten a sour relationship."

"And you know my relationship with Marge has never really been sweet." Sadie shook her head. "But this time…this time it was different. I've never seen Marge so upset. She actually yelled at me."

Edwin squeezed Sadie's hands again, then pulled away and leaned back. "As hard as it is, sometimes taking the first step is actually the best way to soften a hard heart. Even—no, especially—when you're not the one at fault."

Sadie chuckled. "I suppose a slice of humble pie isn't the end of the world."

Apologizing to Marge wasn't going to be easy. But at least she'd know that she had done her part and tried to make amends. Maybe that was going to have to be enough for now. While she couldn't control Marge's actions, she could control her own.

Gloria Garza, owner of Los Pollitos, walked up to their table and set a basket of chips in front of them along with a bowl of salsa.

"Hello, Sadie. Edwin."

"Hi, Gloria," Sadie said, smiling up at her friend.

Gloria worked the front room of the restaurant, occasionally taking orders when things were busy, while her husband, Ramon, did most of the cooking.

Gloria tapped her pen against her order pad. "Interested in today's special?"

"We sure are," Edwin said.

"Absolutely," Sadie agreed.

Gloria walked toward the kitchen to put in their order, and Sadie found herself relaxing as Edwin shared with her one of the issues he was dealing with at his office.

"Do you think the city council will go along with your cuts?" Sadie asked.

"Budget planning always means a little give-and-take, but in the end I know we all just want the best for the city." Edwin laughed. "But that doesn't always make it easy. Especially when you're the mayor."

"No kidding," Sadie said. "By the way, Roz and I went to visit James Abbott. He's the guy who ran the estate sale where Roz picked up that chess set."

"From the Solomon family?"

"Yep. He mentioned hearing that they were involved in some shady things, going all the way back to Prohibition and later with the Mountain Mafia."

"That wouldn't surprise me." He leaned forward. "It's not something you hear much about anymore, but I suppose every town has a few stories they'd rather not publish in the tourist brochure. I mean, not only was there a lot of bootlegging going on during Prohibition, but the Mountain Mafia definitely made their mark in the area as well," Edwin said. "What exactly were you thinking he might be able to tell you?"

"To be honest, I wasn't sure. All I know is that there has been a string of strange things happening, and I'm not the only one who'd like to know what's going on."

"You know who you also should talk to?" Edwin said.

"Who's that?"

"Harry Polmiller. We both know he's a great source of local folklore. You mentioned hearing about some shady things going on at that house in the past, and while you're undoubtedly the expert historian of this town"—he winked—"there's a chance Harry would have some details to add that might help you think through the origin of the chess set and why someone would want to steal it. Even if it does feel like a long shot, it couldn't hurt to ask."

Sadie placed her napkin on her lap as Gloria headed their way with their lunch. "That's a great idea. I'll find some time to stop by tomorrow. Even if it has nothing to do with the chess set, I'm always interested in learning more about our town's history, even the ugly parts."

9

On Monday morning, Sadie took Edwin's advice and headed out to Harry Polmiller's house while Julie watched the store. The questions that had surfaced over the past few days continued to churn through her mind.

Throughout history, Colorado had made a reputation for itself from its spectacular scenery and stories of cowboys and miners. But like any town, there were also a few stories of a devious few with less-than-stellar reputations. There were gangs that robbed banks, even some brothels that ran long ago. Miners had also been entertained by and lost their earnings in gambling halls and saloons. Many of these buildings now served today's tourists and shoppers along Silver Peak's picturesque Main Street.

While Silver Peak wasn't typically mentioned in the roundup of shady towns, Sadie knew there were stories most people had chosen to forget. What she needed was someone who had heard details about those stories firsthand, and Harry Polmiller had been around long enough that he could be the perfect candidate.

Sadie pulled up in front of Harry's modest house, where he grew one of the biggest vegetable gardens in town. She knew of several people who had moved into the area, then went straight to Harry for advice on how to garden at such high altitudes. And Harry always seemed to enjoy both the company and handing out advice.

When no one answered the front door, Sadie found Harry behind his house crouched in his garden, soaking up some of the last sunny days of the year before winter hit. "Harry?"

"Hi, Sadie!" Harry offered her a broad smile. "It's always good to see you."

"I thought you might be working out here."

Harry pulled off his gardening gloves and held out his weathered hand to shake hers.

"How are you, Harry?"

"Getting a tad slower, but I say that every year." He rested his hands against the sides of his slightly hunched form. "I've always said there's nothing like gardening to keep the joints from stiffening."

"You're amazing, and your garden... even this time of year it looks fantastic. I have to admit that sometimes I regret not taking the time to have a large garden."

"It does take a lot of time." Harry shoved his gloves into his pockets, then motioned for her to sit down on one of the chairs at the edge of the garden. "Can't begin to tell you how many newcomers to these mountains have trouble getting plants to live. They try to do things the same way they did wherever they come from, where all you have to do is stick the plant in the ground and wait a few weeks for it to grow. Most of them give up."

"I don't blame them," Sadie agreed. "You and I both know that gardening at this altitude simply isn't the same."

"That's for sure. The sun's intense, the humidity's low, the growing season's short. Especially up here."

"What are you growing now?" Sadie asked, sitting down in the offered wrought-iron chair.

Harry looked out over his large garden with the majestic mountains looming above it in the distance. "With the first frost on its way anytime now, everything I've planted recently has to be able to tolerate the colder weather. From now until mid-January, I'll be growing the more hardy vegetables like spinach, beets, onions, and winter lettuces."

"You've got a gift, Harry."

"You're not the only one who appreciates my hard work." Harry laughed. "My grandson came by to help me with my greenhouse a few days ago. Needed to do some reinforcing to keep out those pesky pocket gophers who think they can live off my gardening. Even put in a short eighteen-inch fence to keep them out, but they still manage to sneak in and steal my stuff."

Sadie laughed with him. "I remember my father telling me what a challenge those critters can be. He used to fight them as well."

"I'm certain anyone who's tried their hand at gardening in these mountains will have quite a few stories to tell." Harry let out a low whistle. "I've had twenty feet of collards simply vanish into thin air due to those gophers. The only sign that anything was wrong was the pile of dirt and, of course, the missing plants."

Sadie's eyes widened slightly. Sounded a little like what was happening at Putnam & Sons.

"I was wondering if I could ask you a few questions about Silver Peak and its past."

"You're the historian, Sadie," Harry said. "Not sure if I know anything you don't already. 'Course, my advanced age might give me some advantage, I suppose." He winked.

"Oh, Harry. You're one of the most youthful people I know." Sadie laughed.

Harry laughed along with her. "So how can I help?"

"Well, you see, it has to do with some missing things, though I wish I could blame it all on a pocket gopher."

"What's gone missing?"

"Among a few other things, a chess set, to be exact. One hand-carved by one of the Solomons back around World War I."

"Ah...the Solomon family." Harry nodded. "Went to school with one of their boys before they moved away from town. They lived in the Browning House for years."

Sadie shifted in her chair and looked at Harry. "Danny Solomon died recently. His granddaughter's in town, planning to get the house ready to sell."

"I'm sorry to hear that. I remember him as a boy."

"What do you remember about him?"

"He was quite a bit younger than I was. Always seemed to have a lot of energy. His father and grandfather were both quite wonderful craftsmen when it came to wood carving. Lost track of the family after they moved away, though I remember they kept the house and rented it out all these years."

"Do you remember when the family left Silver Peak?" Sadie asked.

"Danny must have been about...seven or eight, if I remember correctly." Harry glanced up at her. "Why all the questions, Sadie? You mentioned something was missing?"

"There've been some strange things happening that have sparked my curiosity about the town and its past, though to be honest I'm not sure exactly how any of it is related, or what it is I'm looking for."

All she had was the missing chess set. An old, run-down house. The Solomon family with presumed ties to the local mafia that had once affected even a small town like Silver Peak. But how it all tied together, or what or if it had to do with Roscoe's store, she had no idea.

"You mentioned a chess set?"

"That's part of it. A bit like your collards, it vanished from Putnam & Sons."

"I read in the *Chatterbox* about a ghost at the hardware store."

"You read the *Chatterbox*?" Sadie suppressed a laugh, though in reality it shouldn't surprise her that Harry used the Internet. The *Chatterbox* was an anonymous gossip and news blog Sadie enjoyed reading that focused primarily on the social events in Silver Peak. The author, though, had somehow managed to remain anonymous. The blog kept up with news about weddings, births, and deaths of former Silver Peak residents and their families. And then, of course, there was the local gossip thrown in that Sadie always found amusing and witty. "I haven't looked at the blog in the past couple of days, but I can't say I'm surprised. Of course, we all know that it wasn't a ghost who has been stealing from Roscoe."

"I also read that the sheriff thinks the thefts are tied in with the thieves who have been hitting this area the past few months," Harry said.

"That is his working theory."

"But you don't agree?"

"I'm not sure. But it doesn't seem to fit. Whoever's been breaking into the hardware store has been taking small things, inexpensive things, over a period of weeks—until the other night, when they took the chess set, which really wasn't that valuable either. Or at least not expensive, anyway."

"That is strange."

"What do you remember about the Solomon family?" Sadie asked, ready to delve into the real reason she was here.

"Not a whole lot, not firsthand." Harry clasped his gnarled hands together on his lap and leaned back. "But I heard more stories than I could begin to recount from both my father and my grandfather. There was nothing they liked more than swapping stories, primarily about the silver rush that my grandfather had been a part of. There were countless men who left everything to come during the peak of the silver boom and other gold rushes across the state and country. Some went away wealthier than they ever imagined. Others went away penniless."

"And your grandfather?"

"He arrived at the beginning of the silver boom and happened to be one of the lucky ones. He didn't strike it rich, but he made enough to be able to settle down and start a business up here in these mountains." Harry leaned back in his chair. "I remember him telling me about the hoax at Mount Pisgah where three con men salted gold, planted a fake claim sign, and called the press. Caused quite a commotion, as you can imagine."

"Sounds like one of the darker sides of the silver boom."

Harry laughed. "You probably know quite a bit about this, but there definitely was a dark side. Along with the wealth came a rash of saloons, dance halls, and red-light districts. In the end, production waned along with the dwindling price of silver and most of the mines closed down. The number of full-time residents dwindled, and Silver Peak had to reinvent itself to keep afloat. Of course, we're doing pretty well now."

"What about those who did stick around, after the silver industry collapsed? Like your grandfather, specifically."

"They continued to try to build up the town, though it was never the same—at least population-wise. At the height of the boom the population swelled to over fifty thousand. Today, as you know, it's under six thousand. But that boom resulted not only in an increase in the population, but also in the wealth of the state. Especially here in these mountains. It drove the building of structures in cities and towns and helped to increase the railway network across the mountains, including the narrow gauge line that leads to Leadville. Ended up saving some towns, like Aspen, but in the end, the collapse of the silver prices changed everything. Mining camps became ghost towns. Thankfully, that didn't happen to Silver Peak, though after the devaluation of silver there came issues of probation along with the Mountain Mafia."

"What can you tell me about that time period?" Sadie asked. Harry was right, Sadie *had* studied the era quite a bit, but sometimes anecdotal history was better and more interesting than the history books.

"Prohibition doesn't seem to be something people talk about anymore. There were gambling rackets and crime bosses, especially in the year following Prohibition. Mostly down in southern Colorado, but Denver had its own mob and Silver Peak had its own share of unsavory characters. There were death threats for money. Bootlegging during the Depression. People were pretty much desperate to make money and they found ways to do so in rather...unscrupulous ways. I remember hearing my father telling a few outlandish stories, but at the time I thought he was making up most of them."

"What about here in Silver Peak?" Sadie asked.

"Well, for instance, you mentioned Putnam & Sons. If I remember correctly, the previous owners of that building were connected with not just the bootlegging of alcohol during Prohibition, but they were involved with the Mountain Mafia as well. There was a lot of money to be made by those willing to work outside the law."

Sadie leaned forward. "What else do you remember?"

"I was born at the beginning of Prohibition, so I don't know anything firsthand, but I do know that there was a lot of money at stake. Some of those gangs who set up smuggling alcohol across the country and even on the ocean made massive profits."

"Like Al Capone."

Harry nodded. "Of course, you know how rumors spread, but beneath every tall tale is usually a bit of truth."

Sadie spent a few more minutes enjoying another one of Harry's stories before telling the elderly man she was going to have to leave. She thanked him for his time, gratefully accepted his gift of freshly picked tomatoes, then said good-bye. She was still sorting through what he'd told her when her phone rang as she was getting into her car.

She pulled it out of her purse and answered. "Hey, Roz. What's up?"

"Hungry?" Roz asked.

Sadie laughed at her friend's direct manner. "Getting there." Sadie glanced at the digital clock on the dashboard. It was ten thirty, still a bit early for lunch, but that would give her just enough time to stop by the library. Then this afternoon she'd have to concentrate on Marge's furniture. "Want to meet me at the library first?"

"Of course. Does this have anything to do with the muddy footprints?"

"Maybe. That's kind of what I want to figure out. I'm leaving Harry's house now and, as I expected, he gave me some interesting things to think about. Though, to be honest, I still have far more questions than answers."

10

Sadie headed down Main Street toward the Silver Peak library. The previously multiuse building had been renovated a few years before, making it the most modern building in town. Sadie walked inside, where the library was just as impressive, boasting gorgeous high ceilings, light oak woodwork, and local artwork that lined the walls.

Sadie waved at Kimama, the town's librarian, who was working behind the front desk helping a patron. Kimama was not only an expert in local literature, but she was about as resourceful a person as one could find. Sadie found her creative approach to the work of a librarian inspiring.

Sadie started toward the stairs to join Roz, then paused. Behind a stack of books at the far side of the main room sat Ashley King. Deciding to say hello to the young woman, she slipped past several individuals reading on comfortable chairs or studying at tables.

"Ashley?" Sadie slid into a chair beside the young woman, keeping her voice low. "I thought that was you back here."

"Morning, Sadie." Ashley closed the book she was reading, her finger marking her place, and smiled back. "How are you?"

"Fine, thanks. And you... are you making any progress on the house?"

"It's slow and steady, but yes. My uncle had to go back to Pueblo for the day, so I decided to take the morning off and walk around a bit. Silver Peak is absolutely charming."

Sadie smiled. "I'm a bit biased, of course, but I definitely agree."

Ashley sat back in her chair and glanced at Sadie. "The Victorian-style houses, the opera house and, of course, the mountains in the background. I even splurged on a stack of blueberry pancakes for breakfast at Flap Jack's. It reminded me of Saturday mornings with my mom. She always made us pancakes with real maple syrup." Her expression turned wistful. "Part of me wishes I could just stay."

"I've always believed that a little mountain air can do wonders for the soul."

"I agree. I grew up mostly in Seattle, so this... this is so different. No smog, no traffic jams, and people actually say hello to you and greet you on the streets." Her shoulders relaxed slightly. "My favorite spot, I've decided, is Centennial Park. I love all the trees and the walking trails. I've found it's the perfect place when you need to get away and think."

"You've described Silver Peak to a tee. Fresh air, cold winters, warm, sunny summers, all surrounded by some of the best scenery in the world along with some of the best people as well."

Ashley added the book she'd been reading to the stack in front of her. "You said you'd lived here your entire life. Did you ever consider leaving?"

Sadie glanced at the book's title, her curiosity rising. *Treasure Hunting in the American West* wasn't your typical read. Especially, she assumed, for someone Ashley's age. And she hadn't forgotten that Ashley, more than anyone she knew at the moment, had motivation for stealing the chess set. Which meant that as improbable as it might seem, she definitely wasn't ready to dismiss the idea completely.

"To be honest, I can't imagine living anywhere else," Sadie said, finally answering her question. "We might not have all of the conveniences of a big town, but you really don't have to look far to find everything you need. A grocery store, coffee shops, restaurants, our community church, and even this library."

"I met Fred this morning at Bless Our Souls Jewelry. He and his wife, Debbie, were opening up their shop as I was walking by, and they invited me in." Ashley pulled back her hair to reveal a pair of sunburst chandelier-style earrings. "I love jewelry, especially big earrings, and I couldn't resist these. Aren't they adorable?"

"They are." Sadie chuckled at the younger woman's enthusiasm. "Fred and Debbie are children of the seventies. Straight out of the hippie days."

"Is that their real last name? Sunshine?"

"No, it's Munch," Sadie said, "but they changed it when they were first married."

Ashley laughed. "Sunshine fits them much better."

"I agree," Sadie said. "Are you regretting your decision not to stay?"

Ashley's earrings bobbed as she shook her head. "As much as small-town living tempts me, for now I just plan to finish the house while soaking up as much of the scenery as I can. Like this place. I've never been able to resist a library. And this one is charming."

"Knowing you like to read, I'm sure our librarian would be happy to get you a library card." Sadie pointed to Kimama, who was chatting with someone behind the front desk. Sadie caught the frown on the young woman's face. "But," she prompted the younger woman, "I can tell there's something wrong with that idea."

"I don't know. I signed with a Realtor yesterday, Mary Simpson, but I could tell she was hesitant when she came to look at the property. She explained very clearly that we'd have to find the right buyer—one who is willing to invest in the property—and that won't necessarily be easy."

"Mary's very good at what she does, and she has quite a reach of potential buyers."

Ashley sighed. "I hope you're right. In the meantime, she gave me a list of basic repairs I need to make—in connection with your suggestions—that will help to make the house more sellable. The problem is, Uncle Adam won't be able to stay away from his office much longer, and I certainly can't afford to stay. We'd like to finish up by the end of the week and head back home after that."

"If you need anything in the meantime, please let me know."

"I will. And thank you." Ashley gathered up her bag, leaving the stack of books she'd collected on the table. "And by the way, I haven't forgotten about bringing those books over to your shop...I just haven't had a moment. But I'll be in soon."

"Anytime."

At that, Ashley left.

"Sadie?"

Sadie turned around and smiled up at Anthony, the assistant librarian.

"Hey, Anthony."

"I saw you talking to the woman who just left." Anthony said with his telltale English accent. He pushed back his glasses, which had slipped to the end of his nose. "Do you know her?"

"Her name's Ashley King. She just inherited the Browning House from her grandfather."

"Seems like a sweet girl."

Sadie smiled at Anthony, getting his drift. He was a handsome bachelor, and Ashley was a pretty young woman. "Unfortunately she's not planning to stay around."

"That's too bad, though her taste in books is interesting. She asked what we had on the local mafia, organized crime, and treasure hunting."

Sadie picked up the book Ashley had been reading, still curious over the woman's choice of books. "This looks like an intriguing read. Did she say what she was researching?"

"No, only that she was interested in the history of this area. Of course, I don't know about you, but when I think about the history of Silver Peak and the surrounding area, I typically think of things like prospectors and mining... not organized crime."

Sadie chuckled. "I thought the same thing."

Anthony glanced back at the front desk. "Anything I can help you with before I go back up front?"

"Not at this moment. I'm supposed to meet Roz upstairs. But I'll let you know if I need anything."

"I saw her head up there a few minutes ago. Doing a little research?"

"Yes, actually. You heard about the break-ins at Putnam & Sons? The sheriff thinks it could be connected to the thieves that have hit the area. We thought we'd find out more about them."

"I did hear that, and I find it quite worrisome. But unless they want to add a bunch of books to their stash, I suppose I don't have to worry about them breaking in here."

Sadie found Roz in the microfilm room and sat down in the empty space beside her. "Sorry I'm late. I ran into Ashley downstairs. She was taking a break from working on the house and spent some time walking around town."

"What was she doing at the library?" Roz asked.

"A little research of her own, apparently. According to Anthony, she was interested in the history of Silver Peak, but she was also looking at some books on organized crime in the area, as well as treasure hunting."

"Treasure hunting?"

"Interesting, isn't it?" Sadie shrugged. "She told me she was just interested in learning more about the area, though I can't help but wonder if there isn't something else she's after."

"Like what?" Roz asked.

"That is the question of the day." Sadie glanced at the computer. "Have you found out anything yet?"

"I quickly read through a few articles about the recent robberies on the Internet. They've hit twenty stores in the past two months, and the police still have no idea who they are." Roz shot Sadie a sheepish grin. "But then I decided to come up here and I got a little sidetracked."

Sadie laughed. "Why am I not surprised?"

"I'm not surprised you're not surprised," Roz said with a chuckle. "So what'd Harry tell you?"

Sadie recounted the stories she'd heard from Harry, including the possible link between the Mountain Mafia and Roscoe's store.

How that fit with the break-ins at Putnam & Sons, she could only guess, but perhaps the new band of thieves knew something they didn't.

"And I still have no idea what all this has to do with the chess set—or with Ashley," Sadie said. "If anything."

"But it all feels too coincidental to ignore," Roz affirmed.

"Exactly. I mean, let's walk through it. You bought the chess set at Ashley's grandfather's estate sale. You gave it to Roscoe, who had been experiencing minor thefts in his store. He put the chess set in his shop, it got stolen, and the next day, Ashley called James to make a claim for it."

"It's really bizarre."

"It is. And I have no idea what it means."

"Well, maybe we can find out. If the previous owners of the building were connected with not just the bootlegging of alcohol during Prohibition, but with the Mountain Mafia as well, maybe there's something about the store itself that interests the Mountain Mafia."

"That's an interesting thought. Harry also mentioned what we already know, which is that back in those days, a lot of money could be made by those willing to work outside the law."

"*Hmm,*" Roz said. "Could that, somehow, be tied to present-day treasure hunting?"

Sadie shrugged. "Maybe. Let's just start searching for articles around that time, and see if anything stands out."

Soon Sadie was scrolling through headlines and lead articles from the mid-1920s. She quickly got swept up in it, as she often did when researching days long past. As she read, she saw an op-ed about the end of the war, when the mood across the nation rose along with the demand for liquor. The piece said that there were those who jumped on the opportunity for financial gain despite the laws banning the sale of alcohol. Instead, bootleggers, illegal alcohol traffickers, along with speakeasies spread across the country like a plague, the writer said. Sadie couldn't help but notice the "extra! extra!" tone of the piece.

Another article showed speculative graphs on how many bars and saloons had officially closed their doors, but in reality, had gone underground. The article said they'd appeared in people's basements and attics, businesses disguising themselves as cafés and soda shops, when they were in fact selling illegal alcohol. One graph showed that for every legitimate bar that closed, a half-dozen illegal gin joints were speculated to have opened: around a hundred thousand in New York City and New Jersey, and so on across the entire country, especially in boomtowns. Sadie found a controversial "Style" article that showed an illustration of the latest fashions, which included being seen with a law-eschewing hip flask.

Sadie read on, about Al Capone in Chicago, the Purple Gang in Detroit, Lucky Luciano in New York, and, indeed, the Mountain Mafia, which had spread out across the Rockies. The majority of the speakeasies were controlled by organized crime, and despite the constant raids by law enforcement, the "good guys" were unable to keep up. Or they took paid-out profits and police officer corruption skyrocketed. Not even Silver Peak was isolated from the problem.

She flipped to another article. Probation started early in Colorado, but by the mid-1920s, the public's opinion on Prohibition was beginning to change, as people realized it cost the country both jobs and tax revenues. By the early 1930s Prohibition was on its way out and in 1933 it ended.

Roz nudged Sadie with her elbow. "Look at this. There was a big standoff with the police on Main Street right here in Silver Peak over a large sum of stolen money. Looks like a police officer was killed."

Sadie leaned over and read the article out loud.

A Silver Peak deputy was killed Saturday night after being shot during a raid on Main Street. Deputy John Michael, known by his family as Duke, is the latest person to die in what lately has become far too common. The last incident was in Denver when four officers were wounded and two killed.

According to the local sheriff, three deputies raided one of the businesses on Main Street and found over twenty thousand dollars worth of illegal spirits. There was also a large amount of cash purported to be missing from the premises. Authorities have not identified the shooter, though he is believed to be Louis Solomon of Silver Peak. They are making every effort to find the man responsible. The money in question has not been found.

"Louis Solomon?" Sadie's eyes widened. "That's Ashley's grandfather. The one who made the chess set."

"And we can now connect him to a large—missing—stash of cash. But how does any of this connect to what's going on at Putnam & Sons today?"

"I still don't know," Sadie said, "but I couldn't helping noticing that the showdown took place on Main Street."

11

At five o'clock, Sadie locked up her shop for the day. While progress on the bedroom set had been significant—thanks to Julie, who'd covered for her most of the day at the store—Sadie still wasn't sure if she'd be able to meet Marge's deadline. More than likely she'd need to plan a few long evenings. Tonight, though, she was looking forward to a long walk with Hank before it got dark.

Before she headed home, Sadie had promised to meet Roz and Theo at the hardware store to go over their video surveillance footage again. So far, Theo's plan to catch their thief red-handed hadn't worked, but in her opinion it was still worth pursuing. And since Theo's aging silver Grand Am was parked on the other side of Main Street, it was safe to assume her grandson was already at the store.

Laura Finch, Sadie's paternal cousin who lived in the third-floor apartment above the Antique Mine, called out to her from down the sidewalk, just as she started toward the hardware store.

Sadie stopped to greet the woman. "Hey, Laura. How are you?"

"Hi Sadie, I'm doing great, thanks. I've been swamped at work, so I just ran out to grab some dinner before I get back to it."

Before moving to Silver Peak, Laura had worked in public relations and advising local political campaigns, and now was able to continue her work by telecommuting.

Sadie glanced at the grocery bag Laura was holding. "Something smells delicious."

"Picked up a handmade sandwich for dinner from the Market. I'm on a kick lately with their food."

"Sounds yummy." Sadie slipped the store key into her purse. "I might have to rethink the leftovers sitting in my fridge I'd planned to eat this evening."

Laura laughed. "Are you on your way home?"

"Yes, as soon as I stop by Roscoe's." Sadie started to tell Laura about their "stakeout," then decided there was no reason she needed to worry the woman over the recent break-ins if she didn't already know.

"I was actually planning to drop by the store and talk to you about that," Laura said, "but I ran out of time at work."

Sadie hesitated. "Is everything okay?"

Laura leaned in a bit, as a couple with a small child walked by. "I heard about the break-in at Roscoe's shop. And I saw in the *Chatterbox* that the sheriff is asking everyone to keep their eyes and ears open for anything strange. It got me wondering…and I did think of something odd, though it's probably nothing."

"What is it?" Sadie asked.

"It's Bill Ryder." Laura glanced up at the apartment windows above Putnam & Sons. "He seems like a nice young man, but…"

"But what?" Sadie prodded. Bill was one of Roscoe's renters who had recently moved into the studio apartment above the hardware store.

"I'm honestly not trying to be a nosy neighbor, but I've just noticed he keeps extremely odd hours," Laura said. "He's always going in and out. Sometimes leaving late at night and returning early in the morning. It's probably nothing, but in light of what's going on at the hardware store, it struck me as odd." Laura's frown deepened. "Do you think I should tell the sheriff? Or am I just overreacting?"

"I suppose it wouldn't hurt to tell the sheriff, although I'm not sure that the hours someone keeps is enough to make them a suspect." Still, Sadie filed the information away, should a connection be revealed later.

Laura shook her head and chuckled. "You know, you're right. Forget I said anything. It's probably just me and my overactive imagination."

"No, thanks for telling me, Laura. I definitely think you should run it by the sheriff."

"Will do. Now I'm going to go dig into this Market sandwich. I can't resist Lou's amazing creations."

"What's for dinner tonight?"

"A cowboy tuna melt. I guess the 'cowboy' comes from the fresh green peppers and cheddar cheese."

Sadie's mouth watered at the thought. "Sounds delicious. I just might have to stop by there later."

"Good plan. I'll let you know if it's a total dud, though somehow I doubt it will be."

Sadie laughed. "Always looking out for me, Laura."

"Hey, what are cousins for?" Laura winked, then headed toward their building.

A moment later, Sadie walked into Putnam & Sons, where Roscoe, Roz, and Theo hovered over the computer.

"Did I miss anything?" Sadie asked. "I ran into Laura on the way over."

"Don't worry. Theo's just gotten started," Roz said.

"I just need another couple more minutes," Theo said. He brushed his dark hair back from his eyes and smiled up at Sadie, clearly hoping tonight would be the night they found something.

Sadie turned to Roz while Theo kept working. "Seems like news of the break-in has spread. Laura just mentioned it to me."

"Yeah, I saw Rita this afternoon," Roz said, "and she told me that her brother's leather goods shop in Castle Pines was robbed last Thursday night. The thieves got away with over five hundred dollars in petty cash and even more in merchandise."

"I heard a similar story from Spike," Roscoe said. "He's got a nephew up Highway Sixty-five where thieves struck two nights ago. Broke in through a back window and stole a bunch of valuable car parts. Whoever this gang of thieves is, they've set a lot of people on edge."

"That's what's tripping me up, though," Sadie said. "There just doesn't seem to be any connection with what happened here at the hardware store and what's happening in the surrounding towns." Sadie set her purse down on the counter. "Except for the last break-in here."

"From what I read online," Roz said, "the thieves case the stores, find a vulnerability, then strike at night. Never the same location, and usually never even the same town. They're hitting two, three, even four times a week, and no one has any idea who they are."

Roscoe's gaze shifted to Roz, then back to Sadie. "That might not be true anymore."

"What do you mean?" Sadie asked.

"I went to see the sheriff this afternoon for an update. AJ's Boutique right here in Silver Peak was also hit last night. The thieves stole all their petty cash and a number of expensive cuff links."

"What?" Sadie exclaimed.

"He also told me that they definitely have lock-picking skills, which means they want to take another look at the evidence in my shop, in case they missed something. All I can think of is that maybe they need tools for their operation and that's why they took what they did from my store. But why on earth wouldn't they just purchase them with all the money they've made off with? Seems foolish to risk getting caught just to steal a couple of screwdrivers."

"True. But what about the chess set?" Roz said. "How does that fit in with . . ."

"Wait a minute," Theo cut in. "We've finally got something." He tilted the computer screen so they all could see.

Sadie shifted her focus to the black-and-white image in the left-hand corner of the screen, where Theo was pointing.

"There he is," Theo said, excitement ringing in his voice. "He set off the motion detector."

Sadie, Roz, and Roscoe leaned in closer to the computer monitor, then watched as the shadowy figure crossed in front of the camera holding something in front of his body.

"What is he carrying?" Roz asked.

"Looks like a crowbar," Roscoe said.

"Give me a second. I'll slow down the speed." Theo pointed the cursor to a box in the top left corner of the image and replayed the footage. "It's definitely a crowbar."

Sadie leaned in another couple of inches, trying to make out the form. "Do you recognize the person?"

"It's too hard to see the face," Roz said.

"He's wearing a hoodie," Theo said. "If we could find a clear shot of his face..."

Sadie watched as Theo continued scanning through the footage. All they needed was for their thief to glance up at the camera for just one second and they'd have him.

A moment later, Theo held up his hands and leaned back, disappointed. "I think that's it."

"And we aren't any closer to finding out the identity of who's been breaking in," Roz said.

"At least your ghost theory has been blown," Sadie said. "And I feel pretty certain this person was a male."

Roz laughed. "But he might as well be a ghost! We still have no idea who he is."

Sadie stared at the door of the shop in the video where Theo had frozen the recording. Something still didn't seem right.

"Theo, the camera works as a motion detector, right?"

"Yes."

"Then why don't we see him coming into the store through one of the doors? We only see him exiting. It's as if the first part of the video stream was cut off, and we're missing something."

"Sadie's right," Roz said. "Shouldn't we see him coming in through the door?"

"I suppose it's possible there was a glitch in the recording."

"Can you start at the beginning and replay it one more time?" Sadie asked.

Theo moved the cursor on the screen, then pushed the button to play the recording again.

"He doesn't even go near the front or back doors," Roz said.

"Or the cash register, for that matter."

"I can set it up again tonight," Theo offered. "If he does come back, maybe we can get some better footage this time."

"It's worth a try," Sadie said.

Theo looked disappointed. "I'm sorry this didn't help catch the guy. I was so sure it would work."

"It not your fault," Sadie said. She hated to see her grandson so dejected. "It's a really smart idea, and it might still pan out for us. Let's be sure to tell Mac what we've found. Maybe he'll see something we missed."

12

THE NEXT MORNING, AFTER SADIE'S USUAL WALK WITH HANK, which had included some much-needed prayer time, she drove into town and parked in front of the Antique Mine. Mornings were her favorite part of the day, and this morning she'd gotten up earlier than normal in order to have plenty of time to work on Marge's bedroom set before the store opened at ten.

Julie had promised to come in today, which would give Sadie time to begin the next layer of shellac, but that also meant a trip to Putnam & Sons for some more supplies. She stopped in front of her store with its plate-glass front and looked toward the hardware store. The CLOSED sign was still on the door, and she hadn't seen Roscoe or Roz's vehicle when she'd driven in. She could go ahead and get started with the shellac, then stop by the store later in the morning.

Sadie turned as an old pickup rumbled up beside her and parked. Bill Ryder exited the beat-up vehicle, wearing jeans and a cowboy hat, presumably heading home toward the studio apartment he was renting above Roscoe's store.

"Morning, Bill. How are you doing?"

"Pretty good, Sadie. Thanks."

She liked the young man, although Laura's suspicions replayed through Sadie's mind—along with something else she couldn't put her finger on. Bill seemed tired, but it was more than that. She looked down at his boots. Mud covered the tips.

Sadie glanced back up at his weary expression. "Been out hiking this morning, Bill?"

"Hiking... no... just... just out for a walk," he stammered.

Sadie frowned. Perhaps it was just her imagination, but the man seemed nervous.

"It's a beautiful morning for a walk, even though it is pretty chilly," Sadie said. She wondered for a moment how Harry's garden was taking the cold, then turned her attention back to Bill. "I take my golden retriever, Hank, out every morning along the trails behind my property."

His gaze shifted across the street to the Silver Peak Bank, then back to Sadie. "It is... a beautiful morning, I mean."

What had him so distracted? Was there really something to his odd hours and muddy boots? Sadie wanted to dismiss the thought but she couldn't. Was it possible Bill was somehow involved in the recent string of robberies plaguing the area?

"Is everything all right?" she asked.

"Of course." He shoved his hands into the front pockets of his jeans. "I'm just heading up to my room."

There was something else in his eyes as he looked at her. A sadness. A look of defeat, perhaps. "Are you sure you're okay, Bill?" she repeated.

"Yes, thank you." He started toward the outside door that led to his apartment.

"Did you hear about the break-ins at Putnam & Sons?" she tried a final time to engage him in conversation.

Sadie watched Bill's reaction closely as he stopped and then turned back to her. But as far as she could tell, there was no hint of guilt in his eyes. In Sadie's mind that meant he was either a good actor or he was innocent.

"I did hear about that. It's a shame. I suppose they'll get caught eventually." Bill pulled a set of keys from his pocket. "If you'll excuse me, Sadie, I need to go get ready for work. I'll see you later."

Sadie watched the man disappear into the building. He had seemed unfazed when she asked him about the burglaries, and he certainly hadn't acted guilty. Just because he kept odd hours *and* had mud on his boots didn't mean he was the one who had broken into Roscoe's shop. But it also didn't mean he wasn't.

"Penny for your thoughts."

Sadie nearly jumped as Roz walked up beside her on the sidewalk wearing a colorful blue and green tunic. Sadie pressed her hand against her chest. "You scared me! I didn't hear you coming."

"Don't tell me our ghost has you jumpy," Roz said with a gleam in her eyes.

"Good one." Sadie laughed. "I think we've already proved our ghost is quite human."

Roz followed Sadie toward the front door of her shop.

Sadie wasn't sure how to bring up the subject of Bill, so she figured she'd just take the direct approach. Roz would see through anything else anyway. "So... I just talked with Bill."

"You mean our new tenant, Bill?"

"That's the one. I wasn't sure whether to mention this to you or not, but Laura told me yesterday that she's noticed Bill's been keeping really odd hours—late-night hours. And I just noticed that his boots were muddy."

"Muddy? You mean..."

"The footprints."

"Did you ask him about his boots?"

"Yes. He said he was just out for a walk. And I suppose that's entirely possible. A pair of muddy boots isn't exactly a crime," Sadie said. "And just because the man keeps odd hours doesn't mean he's guilty of something either."

"True, but I do think it's worth mentioning to the sheriff."

"You're probably right. For now, I have to get to work. Otherwise Marge might have my head." She felt bad the second she said it. It wasn't exactly kind of her to perpetuate the idea that Marge was difficult. Marge did that more than enough herself, Sadie thought, then she chided herself again for the ungracious thought.

"And I have a prayer meeting at church," Roz said. "I'll stop by later if I get a chance."

"Sounds good. See you later."

Sadie slipped her key into the front door of her shop. She shivered, and decided to light the stove. Julie wasn't in yet, so she had the quiet shop to herself for the moment.

According to the weather report she'd heard on the radio this morning, winter was on its way and temperatures were starting to drop. While she loved Silver Peak's warm and sunny summers, she was also looking forward to the coming snow that would follow the fall foliage that had the golden aspen trees in full color right now.

She stepped in front of the potbellied stove in the corner of the store, checking to make sure the flue was opened. She grabbed a few sheets of old newspaper next to the stove and wadded several into a small ball before throwing them into the stove. Next she added some oak bark and kindling, along with several larger hickory logs. With a long match, she lit one of the balls of newspaper, then watched the orange and yellow flames come to life.

Sadie stopped in front of the tall, antique walnut locking glass display case where she kept some smaller, more valuable items. Currently there was a row of Depression glass plates, a couple of sterling pennants, a solid silver cutlery set, and a number of rare Matchbox cars from the 1950s she'd recently found at an auction. As far as she knew, nothing was missing in the store, but with what had happened over the past few days, she couldn't help but wonder if she'd overlooked something. She kept going through the facts she knew so far, but the bottom line was, if someone needed cash, why not steal something of value? Why not just break in to her store—or rob the bank for that matter?

Sure, that might be an extreme measure, but Sadie was becoming more and more convinced that there was no connection between the thief at the hardware store and the thieves who had been breaking into shops in the surrounding area.

So what did they want from Roscoe? Perhaps they weren't interested in stealing as much as... Were they *looking* for something? But what about the chess set? Surely the intruder wasn't just a fan of chess and decided to steal it incidentally.

Since nothing of real monetary value had been taken, she had to assume that whatever was happening at Putnam & Sons had nothing to do with money. And that brought her back to

Bill. If he was their mysterious footprint man, why would he just steal a handful of batteries and other miscellaneous things? If he was having money issues and needed cash, was he stealing from Roscoe simply out of convenience? Had he somehow procured a key to the shop?

Just then, Julie arrived. "Hey, friend," she said as she came in. "I can smell the fire... Bless you for starting it."

"I figured we'd need it today." Sadie rubbed her hands together, still trying to get warm. "I could also go for another hot cup of coffee. You?" Sadie had already had a cup this morning during her devotional time, but with the busy day ahead of her, just one cup would never do.

"I'm dying for coffee. How about I run over and get us a cup?"

"Bless *you*," Sadie said with a smile.

Just after Julie walked through the door that connected Sadie's shop with Arbuckle's Coffee next door, the bell ran over the front door jingled, reminding Sadie she'd left it unlocked. She stood up to inform the customer they weren't open yet, then paused at the sight of the sheriff.

"Good morning, Mac. Is everything all right?"

Sheriff Slattery walked in and stopped, hands on his hips, his expression serious. "I'm going around checking on all the businesses this morning to make sure everyone's okay."

"What happened?" Sadie asked.

"The thieves hit Silver Peak again last night."

Concern grew in her gut. "Where?"

"This time, they robbed Bless Our Souls Jewelry."

13

LATER, AFTER MAC HAD TOLD HER AS MUCH AS HE COULD ABOUT the robbery at Bless Our Souls, Sadie was trying to put it out of her head as she worked on Marge's furniture. She hummed along to Hank Williams's recording of "I Saw the Light" playing in the background as she put another coat of shellac on Marge's headboard. It was an appropriate song, for she prayed that God would shed some light on the odd goings-on in Silver Peak, as well as on how to patch things up with Marge Ruxton.

Sadie worked for several more hours, until she started to feel her body giving up on her for the day. She was just starting to clean up the back room when the bell jingled above the front door. Sadie paused in front of the supply shelf, half-expecting it to be Marge. She'd spent extra time in prayer throughout the day just to make sure she kept her attitude in check, because while a part of her wanted to simply avoid the woman, she knew she was going to have to speak to her at some point.

Sadie walked toward the front door, but instead of Marge, it was Ashley standing there.

"Hi, Ashley. How are you?"

"Hi, Sadie. I know it's almost closing time, but this day has been crazy. Do you have a moment to look through these books?"

"Of course, Ashley. I was hoping you'd stop by." Sadie led Ashley toward a sturdy mahogany coffee table and cleared off a stack of vintage magazines.

"Wow. I love this place," Ashley said. "It's so eclectic."

Sadie laughed. "Is that a nice way of saying 'cluttered'?"

"Well, I'll admit I'm not into antiques, but this place definitely has charm," Ashley said genuinely.

Sadie took a peek in the box. "Looks like you've brought with you more than just your grandfather's books."

"I hope you don't mind." Ashley pulled out a wrapped object from the top of the box and started pulling off the packing paper, revealing several glass bottles. "But I found these today and thought you might be interested."

Sadie took one of the bottles from Ashley and held it up to the light. "Wow. These are stunning! Do you know how difficult these are to find?"

Ashley chuckled. "Not a clue. That's why I wanted you to look at them."

Sadie checked the marking on the bottom, feeling like a giddy kid on Christmas morning as Ashley began unwrapping more of them. "These were handblown by Rocky Mountain Bottling Works around the end of the eighteen hundreds. Made right here in Colorado. This one is a handblown druggist bottle with the original paper label...and this one..." She set down the bottle in her hand and carefully picked up another one. "It's a Hutchinson soda bottle. No significant chips, or scratches...or cracks...You'd find these in one of the mining towns, making these an incredible piece of area history."

"I'm assuming they belonged to my grandpa's family, as I'm pretty sure the renters who've lived in the house over the past couple of decades wouldn't have left something like this behind."

Sadie glanced up at Ashley. "Can you think of anyone in your family who might have collected something like this? To be honest, most of them aren't worth a lot money-wise, but they do have historical value."

"My grandma loved old stuff." Ashley's face reddened. "Sorry... I meant 'antiques.'"

Sadie laughed. "No need to apologize. Where exactly did you find these?"

"I found them up in the attic, carefully wrapped away. They must have been there for years. But you don't think they're worth much?"

"Prices will vary greatly, because like every antique, it will depend on a number of factors," Sadie said as she began unwrapping more of Ashley's find and laying them, one at a time, on the antique mahogany table between them. She was completely in her element. "A collector will always look at things like age, condition, color, and historical significance, for example. Bottles made before the turn of the century were all handblown and hand-formed," she continued. "It wasn't until somewhere around 1914 that they began mass-producing the bottles with a machine. Those manufactured bottles have little value to most collectors because of that."

"And the color?" Ashley asked. "Some of these blues and greens are stunning."

"Yes, they are. The most common color, as you can see here, is a light greenish-blue. Next you have a lot of amber and clear bottles. Cobalt is normally in demand, unless it's a common bottle like a Bromo-Seltzer one, which would only sell for a few dollars." Sadie set the bottle she was holding back in the box, certain she'd have no trouble finding the perfect buyer for the lot. "The local drugstore back then would have held most of these, both for medicine and for syrup to make sodas.

"Looks like there are also quite a few medicinal whiskey bottles in here as well," Sadie continued. "These would have been sold by a local drugstore during the Prohibition years as a way to get around the alcohol ban. And"—Sadie held up another bottle—"notice that it has never been opened. It's pretty rare to find an unopened whiskey bottle, since most of these were bought with a prescription, then consumed.

"Beyond what you see here, back in that time there were fruit jars; barber and hair bottles; soda, spring water, and apothecary jars; and of course, reproductions of all of these that might not be easily recognized by a noncollector"—Sadie started carefully rewrapping the whiskey bottle—"but they would be easy for a collector to identify. There are also certain geographical areas that have bottles that are in higher demand. The Rhode Island Hutchinson soda bottles, for example, are in demand, along with drugstore bottles embossed with the word *Territory*."

Sadie placed the unopened whiskey bottle back in the box and glanced at Ashley. Clearly the young woman wasn't interested in antiques. The only reason she was here, in fact, was because she needed money. Fortunately both the bottles and the books, given the right buyer, could bring in a fair share of cash.

"That's interesting." Ashley said politely, then hesitated. "My mother would want me to keep all this stuff. She loved books. But I also think she'd understand that I need the money right now."

"Are the two of you close?" Sadie asked, hoping her question wasn't too personal.

"We were." Ashley's voice cracked as her smile faded. "She died a few months ago."

"Oh, Ashley...I'm so sorry."

"Me too. Thanks, Sadie. I don't want to keep you much longer." Ashley attempted a smile.

"Not at all," Sadie replied warmly. "It will take me some time to go through all this and verify its worth, but when I'm finished you'll be the first to know."

"That sounds great." Ashley reached for her purse. "I'll be here at least through the end of the week working on the house."

The thought again occurred to Sadie that, more than anyone else she could think of, Ashley had motivation to steal the chess set. But why would she take the trouble to steal it if there was the possibility it was already rightfully hers? And why call and make a claim on it the day *after* she stole it? Maybe Sadie could find a way to delicately ask Ashley about it. But she'd have to think fast.

"Actually, Ashley, there is something else I need to ask you about before you go," Sadie said. James had called earlier in the day, after finally being able to confirm that the chess set had been on the list of things left to Ashley. "I had a chance to speak with James Abbott today."

"Oh? I spoke with him as well, actually." A shadow crossed Ashley's face. "I had hoped my grandpa had left his chess set to me. It was really special to me. I guess that's part of why I wasn't thrilled about the books, now that I think about it."

Maybe they were finally getting somewhere. "How do you mean?"

"Well, what I really wanted was that chess set. It was made by my great-great-grandfather and eventually passed down to my grandpa. He's the one who taught me how to play chess." A smile played on her lips. "We used to sit for hours in his living room with the board between us. The first time I beat him, I was convinced I was a genius."

"That's such a sweet memory, Ashley."

She smiled. "It is. I miss him."

"Tell me about him," Sadie prompted. If there was something valuable about the chess set, perhaps Ashley knew something. "Seems like you two were close."

Ashley's smile lit up her face. "As a child, I loved spending time with him. Like his own grandfather, he was a master at making puzzles, primarily wooden ones, and he loved riddles. We lived close to each other until my mother got a job back East, and we had to move away. At least that's what she always told me, but I knew it was more than that. I used to write him letters and I never understood why he never wrote me back. After my mother died, I found the stack of letters I thought I'd sent to him. She never mailed them."

"Do you know why she wanted to cut off contact with him?"

Ashley shrugged. "She told me one time that my grandpa was involved in some kind of criminal activity and she didn't want him to be a bad influence on me, though I never believed her. After my mom passed away, I planned to reconnect with her father. By the time I found him, though, he'd passed away."

"That must have been hard on you."

"It was."

"I have no doubt." Sadie paused. "You remember my friend Roz?"

"Of course," Ashley said.

"She's actually the one who bought the chess set at the sale. It was a gift for her husband…"

Ashley straightened up in her chair, eyes wide. "Then she has my grandpa's chess set?"

"Well, no." Sadie hesitated.

"I don't understand."

"Roz's husband, Roscoe, set it out at his hardware store for customers to play with each other. Someone broke in and stole it."

"You're kidding! I know about the break-ins, but I hadn't heard that. Why would anyone want to steal an old chess set?"

Sadie shook her head at the question. "I don't know."

"I only wanted it because of the sentimental value and the fact that my great-great-grandfather had carved all the pieces." Ashley reached for her purse again and shook her head. "I've taken up far too much of your time already and shouldn't be bothering you with this."

"Please don't feel bad. I'm glad you came by."

A moment later, Sadie shut the door behind Ashley and flipped the sign to CLOSED. Ashley had seemed genuinely surprised when Sadie told her about the theft. But if Ashley hadn't stolen the chess set, then who had?

14

WEDNESDAY MORNING, SADIE PULLED INTO MILO HENDERSON'S horse ranch, just a half mile from her own house. The Hendersons owned the prosperous ranch and they boarded horses there, including Scout, Sadie's five-year-old chestnut gelding. With winter clearly on its way, Sadie wanted to take advantage of the crisp, sunny morning for some early riding and exercise before the snow came. And with no school today, her grandkids were planning to meet her here this morning too.

Sadie exited her car, then headed for the barn, which fit in perfectly with the white picket fence, open pastures, and mountains in the background.

"Hey, Sadie."

Sadie walked over to the truck as the rancher pulled to a stop. "Morning, Milo."

"Off for a ride?"

"School's closed for a professional development day for the teachers, so I'm meeting Theo and Sara. They should be here in the next few minutes."

"It's the perfect day for a ride. I'd be out there as well, except I'm on my way into town to meet Wyatt for breakfast. Jenna and

Caleb are visiting her parents and Wyatt . . . well . . . he seems a little lost without her, you know? Thought he could use some company and a big plate of food." Wyatt, Milo's younger brother, was married to Jenna, and Caleb was their two-year-old son.

"Somehow I'm not surprised. Jenna does spoil him." Sadie laughed. "How long is she going to be gone?"

"Just a few more days, thankfully." Milo rested his hands on the steering wheel. "By the way, I've just hired an extra hand to help around the ranch and get things ready for winter. He's in the barn now replacing one of the doors, but I know he'll be happy to help you get the horses saddled up."

"That would be great, Milo. Tell Wyatt hello for me."

"Will do."

Milo shifted the truck into gear, then started back down the drive toward town. Sadie breathed in the brisk mountain air and scanned the captivating scenery of autumn leaves framed by snowcapped mountains in the distance. It was true what she'd told Ashley about the mountain air being good for the soul. Whenever she needed a new perspective on life or just time to think, this was the perfect setting.

Sadie stepped into the barn, the sun casting a streak of light through the entrance. Bill Riley stood there fixing a hinge on the large door.

"Why, Bill, good morning. Milo just told me he'd hired someone new, but I had no idea it was you! I didn't realize you were a handyman."

"Yes . . . I just started a few days ago."

Sadie glanced down at Bill's mud-encrusted feet, puzzled. If this job explained his muddy boots, then why hadn't he just told her the truth?

"My father started out in construction, building houses," Bill began. "Building just about anything, really. When I was a teenager, I used to work with him over the summer. He taught me everything I know."

"I thought you were working in town?" Sadie asked.

"I was...I mean, I am." Bill leaned against the barn wall, frowning, as if choosing his words. "Sadie, you were right. Something has been bothering me since I saw you the other day." He hesitated. "I lied to you. And it's going to sound stupid now that I'm telling you this, but I wasn't really out for a walk around town. I got a job here, and I'd just gotten off of work."

"It's certainly your choice whether to tell me or not, but why the secret?"

"I needed a second job. Milo needed someone to help get the ranch ready for winter, and I'm not bad as a handyman." Bill's gaze dropped to the barn floor. "Truth is, I guess I'm embarrassed. I used to have my own business in Denver and I did quite well, actually. Took over my father's business selling RVs, boats, and motorcycles, but over the last couple of years, things have gone downhill. The recession hit, which meant people aren't buying as many luxury items, and I eventually lost the business."

Sadie caught the deep look of sadness in the man's eyes. "I'm sorry."

"Me too. My wife filed for divorce, and I...I just needed to get away. Which brought me here—to become a short-order cook along with mucking horse stalls and working as a general handyman. Not that I'm complaining about the work, but it's just that after building up my father's business for so many years...it's embarrassing to realize how I've failed." Bill rubbed the back of his neck. "I guess it seemed easier somehow if no one knew."

Sadie shook her head. "There is nothing to be embarrassed about. I admire a man who works hard and refuses to let life beat him down."

"I wish my wife agreed with you, or shall I say, my soon-to-be ex-wife. She kicked me out after I lost the business. Claims I can't provide for her like I used to. Which is true. But I'm determined to get out of debt. I've also been meeting with Pastor Don. I knew him from Denver. He's the one who encouraged me to move here, at least until I can get my life back on track. And then…I don't know what will happen, but he keeps telling me not to give up."

"Good advice. He's a good man."

"I agree. His sermons are very down-to-earth, and he doesn't mind getting into my business." Bill let out a deep chuckle. "Which is something I clearly need right now."

Sadie was touched by his honesty. "Since we're making confessions, I have one as well."

Bill looked surprised.

"I thought you could have been the one who left the muddy footprints at Putnam & Sons."

Bill glanced down at his muddy boots. "You thought I was the hardware store thief?"

"A lot of strange things have been happening in town," Sadie began, "and with the mud and the strange hours someone said you were keeping…well, I'm sorry for ever doubting you."

"All of that is true. I've been taking every shift available at the restaurant and the rest of my time I've spent working here. Sleep has become a nonessential. Problem is, I'm not as young as I used to be. In college I got by on coffee fumes. Fifteen years later, well…let's just say it's not as easy."

"One thing I've learned over the years, Bill, is that life is full of ups and downs. The good thing about that is that the downs don't last forever. My family once owned a prosperous ranch near here, but during the Great Depression, they were forced to sell off large sections of the land, almost losing everything. They were able to keep a couple of acres, which I'm grateful for. I still live in the old farmhouse."

"Maybe one day I'll be able to start over again and set down roots."

"I hope so, Bill. I really do." Sadie smiled, glad that her first instincts about the man had been correct.

Thirty minutes later, Sadie, Theo, and Sara were headed toward the vast system of trails behind the Henderson Ranch. Horse riding was one of Sadie's favorite getaways, because of the peace and quiet of the mountains. As a history buff, she could almost feel as if she were stepping back into time and seeing the splendor of the Rockies the same way the first settlers had seen it.

"It's beautiful out here, isn't it, Grandma?" Sara whispered as she came up alongside Sadie on the familiar trail. A pair of deer stood not far from where they were.

"Stunning."

They stood still for a few minutes until the deer finally bounded off into the woods, then continued following the narrow trail through the clearing.

"A bunch of guys are planning to spend a weekend up here camping before it gets too cold." Theo finally spoke out loud.

"That sounds like fun," Sadie said.

"We tried to get Ricky Campbell to come as well, but he's got a job on the weekends now."

"Do you know him well?" Sadie asked. Roscoe hadn't mentioned the young man again, but she knew he was concerned Ricky could be behind the thefts at the store. She'd like to know if there was any basis at all to that theory.

"He's in my class at school. We're not like best friends or anything, but we hang out every once in a while."

"And what are your impressions of him?"

Theo leaned forward and rubbed Bronco, his three-year-old black gelding, on the neck as they kept riding. "He works hard at school. He's focused. Quiet. Has always gotten good grades."

"Any extracurricular activities he's involved in?"

"He used to play sports, but I don't think he's planning to play this year."

"Do you know why not?"

Theo shrugged. "I just heard the coach talking to him one day after school. Ricky told him he didn't have time for sports anymore. I figured he was focusing on his grades. You know, hoping to get a good scholarship after he graduates."

Sadie pressed further. "Has he seemed...I don't know... different lately?"

"You know, now that you mention it, I haven't seen him hanging around after school like he used to."

"Do you know why?"

"I heard his mom's pretty sick. He did mention that he had to go to Denver with her for a few days last week."

"Was he back in school this week?"

"Yeah," Theo said.

Sadie gripped the reins more tightly. The fact that Ricky made it back to school meant he probably would have been back in town by Sunday night. Was it possible that Ricky was the one on the footage Theo caught?

"Do you know what's wrong with his mom?"

Theo shook his head. "All I know is that she used to work at the pharmacy, but she had to quit her job."

Sadie nodded, remembering the young woman who was often behind the counter. Mary...Marie? She'd always been professional and friendly, though she never seemed very interested in striking up a conversation. If Ricky's mom was sick, though, it would make sense that he might feel he needed to get an after-school job. But if Ricky's mom was having financial issues, and her son had managed to get a copy of the key, he'd surely be stealing things of value. Not flashlights and batteries.

But did that alone prove the boy's innocence?

During her lunch break, Sadie decided to walk across Washington Avenue to the ABC Pharmacy. As the only chain in town, ABC Pharmacy might be a national brand, but this particular location was special because the staff was as friendly as any local establishment in town.

Sadie walked into the store and headed straight to the back, where Greg normally worked. Thankfully, it didn't look as if there were any customers at the moment.

"Good evening, Greg," Sadie said, stepping up to the counter.

"Sadie. It's good to see you. You're not sick with this cold going around, are you?"

"Thankfully, no. But I do know several people who have come down with it."

"Try to avoid them, then. I can't tell you how many prescriptions I've filled in the past week. Doc's been just as busy, I'm afraid."

"And winter hasn't even settled in yet." Sadie readjusted her purse strap on her shoulder. "I actually stopped by to ask about one of your employees. Or a former employee, rather. Marie Campbell."

Greg leaned forward and rested his hands, palms open, against the counter. "It's a sad story, actually. I hired her a few months ago, after she and her son moved to Silver Peak. At first she worked out fine. She was a great employee. Quick to take the initiative, and a hard worker."

"What happened?" Sadie asked.

"The problem was that while she was always very diligent and nice to the customers, she was also sick a lot. And while I believe her story, I ended up having to get someone more reliable to take her place. I felt bad—I still feel bad, actually—but there wasn't much else I could do."

"That's understandable. Do you know her son?"

"Ricky?" Greg nodded. "He's a good young man who has his hands full with helping his mom, going to school, and I understand he's working in town as well."

Sadie nodded. "He works over at Putnam & Sons."

"I suggested to Marie that they speak to Pastor Don about getting some extra help if they needed it. Especially since she seemed so worried about how all of this was affecting Ricky. To be honest, I'm not sure how she was making it financially."

"What about the boy's father?"

"His parents are divorced, but that's all I know. I never heard Marie talk about him, which gave me the impression he's out of the picture." Greg shook his head. "Why? Is something wrong?"

Sadie paused. The last thing she wanted to do was meddle, but neither could she dismiss the possibility that Ricky was somehow involved in the thefts. "To be honest, I'm not sure at this point."

Sadie thanked Greg for his time, then headed out of the store. Ricky might not seem like the type who would have broken into the hardware store, but now that Ricky was back in town, it was time Roscoe had a heart-to-heart talk with the young man.

15

As soon as she could, Sadie went over to Putnam & Sons to talk to Roscoe about what she'd just learned about Ricky. She waited beside a display of solar lights while he finished up with a customer. While her knowledge of the hardware store's history was limited, she'd heard Roscoe tell numerous stories about his great-grandfather over the years.

Simon Putnam had been an itinerant peddler of hardware goods for the residents of Silver Peak, as well as some of the outlying camps and towns, during the height of the mining boom. Eventually, he was able to settle down and open up a proper store on the other side of town. The business, which saved people from having to go into Denver for supplies, was an immediate success. Later, his son expanded the business even further by moving the store to its current location on Main Street, and now, decades later, business was still thriving.

"Sadie," Roscoe said, pulling her from her thoughts, "sorry to make you wait."

Sadie smiled up at him. "Not a problem, Roscoe."

"Need more supplies for your project?"

"Not at the moment." She clasped her hands in front of her. "I actually came to talk to you about Ricky."

Sadie explained what Theo had told her while they'd been out riding, as well as what she'd found out from Greg at the pharmacy.

"Wow," Roscoe said, leaning against the counter. "I had no idea he was going through so much. I wonder why he didn't just tell me."

"Is he coming in today?" Sadie asked.

"He called to tell me he was back in town." Roscoe glanced at his watch. "He should be here in a little over an hour. He asked to work this afternoon, since school's out for the day. Maybe I should drive up to his place and have a talk with him before his shift starts. Tom can watch the store while I'm out."

"That's not a bad idea," Sadie said.

Roscoe glanced at the door as a customer came in. "Would you mind coming with me?"

Sadie hesitated at the request. "I'm not sure he'd feel as comfortable if I showed up with you."

Roscoe waved away her concern with his hand. "You have a way with people, Sadie, and Roz is out getting her hair done. I guess I'd prefer not to do this alone."

"Of course, then. If you're sure," Sadie said. "You know I'm happy to help if I can."

Ten minutes later, Sadie stepped out of Roscoe's car in front of the cabin where Ricky lived, still feeling like an intruder to the situation. The cabin was a rustic, one-story structure on the edge of a large piece of property that overlooked the mountains. Ricky was out in the front yard raking leaves.

"Afternoon, Ricky," Roscoe said warmly, walking up the driveway.

"Mr. Putnam. I'm not supposed to be at work right now, am I?" Ricky held up the rake beside him, frowning. "I promised my grandfather I'd do some yard work before coming into town."

"No, you're fine. I just wanted to stop by and see how you were doing. Have you met Sadie Speers?" Roscoe asked.

"I've seen you around town," Ricky said, shaking her hand and offering her a slight smile. "It's nice to meet you, Mrs. Speers."

"It's nice to officially meet you as well, Ricky. You probably know my grandson, Theo Macomb."

"Sadie's a close friend of Roz, and she's been helping us try to figure out who's been breaking into the store."

"I heard about that." Ricky leaned against the rake handle. "They still haven't caught anyone?"

"Not yet, I'm afraid."

Ricky leaned the rake against the tree, clearly feeling uncomfortable from the expression on his face, and nodded toward the house. "Do you guys want to come inside? Mom's sleeping, but we could sit in the dining room."

"No, thank you," Sadie offered quickly, not wanting to disturb his mother. "It's beautiful out here." It was a crisp afternoon, the temperature not as cold as the day before, and the sun was bright and warm.

Sadie sat down between Ricky and Roscoe on one of the old garden chairs positioned at the side of the yard where the view of the jagged, snowcapped mountains was the best.

Ricky gripped the arms of his chair, not even noticing the scene as his frown deepened. "Is there a problem?"

"I guess I might as well get right to the point," Roscoe said finally. "About the problem of the thefts at the store . . . "

"Wait." Ricky's eyes widened. "Do you . . . think it's me?"

Roscoe shook his head. "I honestly don't know who it is, but you *have* had access to a key, so, as much as I hate to, I have to talk with everyone who could have gained entry." Roscoe leaned forward and caught Ricky's gaze. "But I *also* know that you're a hard worker and you have never caused me any problems." Roscoe's implication that he believed Ricky was innocent was, Sadie believed, the perfect way to draw out the truth from him, regardless of whether he was guilty.

"Well, I have been struggling to keep up with school." Ricky's hands fiddled with the sides of the chair, but he didn't look away. "But I haven't stolen anything, and I never would. My mom taught me better than that."

"I'm happy to hear that," Roscoe said, shooting Sadie a glance before leaning back.

"So you believe me?"

Roscoe nodded. "Yes, I do."

Ricky let out a deep sigh. "Thank you." Sadie wanted to believe him too. He appeared to be a genuine kid, and academic struggles didn't automatically make someone a thief.

"You said your mom was asleep," Sadie said, knowing his mother was a subject that needed to be addressed as well. "Is she feeling all right? We heard she'd been sick."

"Yeah..." This time Ricky looked away. "It's...well...I hope it's going to be okay. She was diagnosed with chronic fatigue syndrome a few months ago. The doctors still aren't sure exactly what's wrong, but she's tired all the time. It's hard for her to get out and keep a job. That's why we went to Denver this weekend," he admitted. "So she could see a specialist."

"I wish you would have told me all of this," Roscoe said. "I could have adjusted your hours..."

Ricky shook his head. "Actually, Mr. Putnam, that's *why* I didn't tell you. I need the work. I hope you're not planning to cut my hours..."

"I see. No, as long as you feel like you can handle it, the hours are yours."

Sadie caught the look of relief in the boy's eyes and realized what a burden he had to carry. At seventeen, he'd become the man of the family, with responsibilities most kids never had to face. She knew from her own experience how Alice's divorce had changed not only her daughter's life, but Sara and Theo's lives as well. But at least her grandchildren had been able to remain kids, and not worry about having to help support their family.

"Do you have other relatives in the area beside your grandfather, Ricky?" Sadie asked, wondering if there was a way to help this family.

"My father ran off a few years back, so now it's just the three of us. We're okay, but it's been hard with my mom sick and Grandpa's arthritis making it tough for him to get around."

Trying to balance school, work, and taking care of his mom. No wonder his grades had suffered.

"You know you can always come to me about all of this stuff, right?" Roscoe asked.

"I know..." Ricky's face flushed and his hands clenched at his sides. "Thanks...I just didn't want to bother you."

"It's not a bother," Roscoe said reassuringly.

"So I'm not going to lose my job?" The tension in the boy's shoulders and jawline seemed to be relaxing. "I thought you were mad at me. That you thought I stole that stuff..."

"No, Ricky, I don't think you broke in, and I never really did. In fact, if you want to work a few more Saturdays so you can bring in some extra money, I could use the help, as long as you'll try extra hard to keep up with school too. Would that be all right?"

Ricky's smile broadened. "It really would, and I will. Thank you."

Sadie hesitated as the three of them stood up. There was one other thing they needed to ask regarding what had been happening at Putnam & Sons. "I do have one other question before we leave, Ricky," she said.

He put his hands in his pockets and looked up at her. "Sure."

"We still have no idea who has been breaking into the store. I was wondering whether you'd noticed anything strange the past few weeks. Anything that at the time might have seemed a little off, but now, knowing what's going on..."

A cool breeze fluttered the leaves of the maple tree beside them as Ricky thought through the question. "I'm not sure..."

"It could be something simple, like things misplaced or missing on the shelves like I noticed," Roscoe prompted, "or a customer acting strangely..."

"Actually"—Ricky looked up at them—"I forgot about this, but there was a guy who came in...two, maybe three weeks ago. He asked a lot of questions, but he didn't buy anything. And his questions had nothing to do with anything in the store."

"Do you remember what he asked?" Roscoe said.

Ricky shrugged. "He seemed interested primarily in the town's history and the history of the store in particular."

"That *is* odd." Roscoe shook his head. "A hardware store isn't exactly where most people go for tourist information."

"That's what I thought at the time."

"What did you tell him?" Sadie asked.

"That I didn't know much more than that the store had been in the Putnam family for a long time. I told him I'd only lived here a few months and that if he required more information he needed to talk to you, or maybe do some research at the library. To be honest, I really didn't know how to respond. Normally people who come in want a new hammer or a garden hose, not information on the history of the building."

"Do you remember what he looked like?" Sadie asked.

Ricky's mouth twisted slightly. "I don't know. Thirty... maybe forty. Dark, short hair. A couple of inches taller than me. I honestly don't remember more than that."

"That's fine," Roscoe said. "Just let me know if you think of anything else."

"I will." Ricky slapped his palms against his thighs. "And thank you. Both of you."

"You're welcome," Roscoe said as they said good-bye and turned to leave.

Roscoe drove them back toward town down the gravel road lined by golden aspens shimmering in the wind.

He tapped his fingers against the steering wheel. "I can see myself at that age in him. Most kids don't have to deal with balancing school and having to bring home money to help pay the bills."

"I have a feeling he's going to do just fine," she said. "Especially if we can give him some more support."

"I think you're right."

But two questions still remained in Sadie's mind as Roscoe followed the winding road into town. Who had come into the store asking questions about its history? And if Bill, Ricky, and Ashley weren't stealing from the shop, then who was?

16

Sadie spent the rest of the afternoon working on Marge's bedroom set in the back room, while Julie watched the store. With time quickly running out, not only did it allow her to concentrate on the restoration project, but it also gave her time to mull over what had recently been happening in town.

While the local authorities in a hundred-mile radius—including Mac—continued to follow leads on the thefts, so far no one seemed any closer to catching the crooks who had now added Silver Peak to their list of conquests. Neither had anyone been able to conclusively prove if what had happened at the hardware store was connected to the other crimes.

Sadie took a step back, pleased with her progress. She pulled a bright light from one of the shelves, plugged it in, and began examining the surface of the grain, carefully looking for any places she might have missed.

She continued with the process, taking her time to ensure she hadn't missed any spots. Some people preferred to stop after the last layer of shellac was put on, but Jean-Pierre had recommended a final glazing step, and she'd decided to go ahead next with his advice.

"Sadie?"

Sadie flipped off the light and looked up. "Hi, Marge." She could hear the tightness in her voice, even as she tried to sound pleasant. "I didn't hear the bell ring out front."

"I was in town and thought I'd take a moment and stop by." Marge's voice was clipped. Apparently neither of them had gotten over their earlier spat.

Marge started walking slowly around the bed. "I can tell you've made quite a lot of progress, but I have to say. I've been doing some research of my own on refurbishing pieces like this one on the Internet, and frankly, Sadie... I'm not sure this process is right for the bedroom set."

"Not right? I don't understand."

Sadie worked to keep her attitude in check. After hours and hours of Sadie's hard work, Marge was still having second thoughts? She sent up a quick prayer for wisdom on how she should respond to the woman. Because at the moment, the only things that came to her mind weren't exactly Christlike.

"I was surprised to discover that the process you are using makes the wood prone to ring marking and heat marks. I'm also worried that the finished product is going to be too fragile. Because," Marge said, rushing on, "it seems clear that the shellac is much softer than other finishes and there will be a greater risk of water damage."

Sadie glanced at the headboard, which now looked more like frosted glass than the finished glossy surface, but as she'd explained more than once, Marge simply needed to reserve judgment until she was finished.

"While that may be true about the procedure, you told me you wanted the furniture refurbished in a way that was typical of when this bedroom set was made. I explained to you as well that after building up the coat of shellac, I would have to sand out the brushstrokes and other marks."

Marge shook her head. "I'm not sure this was the best choice, though, after all."

"We talked about all of the options before I started, and I mentioned those issues to you. I also told you that this is actually simpler to repair than other finishes."

"That might be true but..."

"All I know to tell you, Marge, is that the process is going well, and the final result is going to be stunning. You just need to trust me."

Marge tapped her forefinger against her lips before responding. "There's also the issue of the color. I'm afraid it's still far too light."

Sadie tried to rein in her brewing frustration. She'd known from the beginning that Roz's warnings had been correct, but she'd seen this project as an opportunity to work on her skills and to give Marge a stunning piece of furniture in the end. To hear Marge's constant complaints—especially at this stage—was simply unacceptable.

Sadie took in a deep breath, then expelled it slowly. "Marge, as I've asked you to do over and over, please trust me. You have yet to see the finished product. As for the color, it's still beautiful. The bottom line, though, is that it's simply too late to change the process at this point."

Sadie stopped, hoping she'd said something to get through to her customer, because arguing with the woman wasn't going to get them anywhere. As the client, Marge did have the final say as to what she liked, because in the end, she was the one who was going to have to live with the piece in her house.

Yesterday, Sadie had even called Jean-Pierre to ask him a few questions regarding the restoration project, and she had been assured she was moving in the right direction. Convincing Marge of that, though, seemed impossible.

"Just let me finish the project," Sadie said once more. Taking the high road and finding a way to apologize and forgive Marge was turning out to be a whole lot harder than she'd expected.

"And if I still don't like it?"

"You still have the old bedroom set, don't you?"

"Well, yes, but..."

"If, by the end of the week, when I'm finished with the process, you still aren't pleased, I'll simply find another buyer who is interested and you'll be free to go to Denver—or wherever—to find something more suitable to your tastes. But as I said, it's too late to start over with this bedroom set at this point."

"I suppose that means I don't have a choice. I was so hoping to have something new by the time my family arrived. Something I liked..." Marge's tone was becoming whiny.

Sadie took a lamp from the shelf, forcing a smile, while the verse about heaping burning coals on your enemy's head through kindness played through her head. "I hope the rest of your day goes well, Marge, but I need to get back to work," she said politely before Marge turned and walked out the door.

Once Marge had left, Sadie tried to concentrate on her work, but something in the woman's words had managed to sap some of the joy out of the process. While Marge had always been a difficult client, today she'd become downright impossible. Without a doubt there was nothing Sadie could do at this point to please the woman.

Deciding all she could do was focus her frustration into something positive, Sadie pulled up a renewed sense of energy and grabbed the shellac pad, determined to give Marge the most beautiful bedroom set the woman had ever seen.

Thirty minutes later, Sadie was just about done when Roz stepped into the back room.

"Roz." Sadie pressed her hand against her heart. "I'm so glad it's you."

"Why? You seem... jumpy. Are you all right?"

"I'm fine." Sadie let out a sigh and kept working. "I just need a few minutes to finish this last layer so it has time to dry overnight."

"I know you're used to working long hours, but you look tired today," Roz said.

"Well, as you warned me, it's been very time-consuming, and Marge's attitude hasn't helped, but I am pleased with the progress. I sent photos to Jean-Pierre this morning. He's been giving me pointers along the way, and he assures me that I'm right on track."

"But something's wrong." Roz moved next to Sadie, her gaze narrowed on her friend's face. "What is it?"

Sadie pressed her lips together. She wouldn't go into the details of Marge's outburst a few days ago, but even Roz knew how difficult it was to please the woman. "You were one hundred percent correct. She came by this afternoon—again—to check on my progress. She's decided after some perfunctory research on the Internet that the shellacking process isn't the right method for this particular bedroom set."

"You're kidding me? What are you supposed to do?"

"That's precisely what I asked her. I can't exactly switch methods at this point. I'm almost finished." Sadie arched her back to try to work out some of the kinks that had settled in while she'd been working. "I agreed with her that there are pluses and minuses to this process, but one of the reasons I chose this method was to stay true to the original finish of these pieces. And that was exactly what Marge asked me to do in the beginning. Or so I thought."

"I'm so sorry."

"I don't regret taking on the project," Sadie said. "Not at all. But you reminded me when I started this project that I would not only have to deal with the refinishing project, but I'd also have to deal with Marge, and *that* is what I regret."

Sadie hesitated. She had no intention to gossip, but she also needed to vent. And she knew Roz was able to keep anything she said confidential. "I just wish I didn't let her affect me so much. I've always been able to get along with most people—and even Marge, for the most part, but lately... I don't know. It's as if she's even more prickly than normal. And on top of that, I'm almost done with the project, trying to meet her self-imposed deadline, and she's doesn't like it."

"What are you going to do?" Roz asked.

Sadie had mulled over her options all week, but as hard as she was trying to truly forgive Marge, after today it seemed clearer than ever that there was nothing she could do to please the woman. Which left her with what she should have done in the first place.

"I'm going to stop by Marge's house tonight and tell her that since it's obvious I can't do the work to her satisfaction, she'll need to find someone else to finish the project the way she wants it done, or buy a different bedroom set."

"I think you're wrong on this one," Roz said. "And I was too."

Sadie turned to her friend. "What do you mean, I'm wrong? You think I should continue?"

"Yes, I do."

Sadie started putting her supplies away. "No, Marge is clearly not happy, and there's nothing I can do or say that will change that."

"Then maybe you need to apply some of the same techniques on Marge."

Sadie glanced up at her friend. Roz never shied away from offering advice or asking personal questions if she thought they were warranted. But Sadie knew she didn't do it to pry, only to help. And when it came to Marge, Sadie needed all the help she could get. Taking the high road seemed noble until you actually had to take it. "I'm not sure I follow you."

"I might be wrong, but I don't think Marge's reaction to your work has anything to do with the bedroom set, how you decided to refinish it, or even with you for that matter." Roz leaned against the worktable. "I read a quote a while back that talked about how we tend to judge *ourselves* by our intentions, but *others* by their actions. So maybe what you need to do is try to find a way to build rapport with Marge. Find something the two of you have in common."

No matter how impossible she might think that was—or as much as she didn't want to admit it—Sadie knew Roz was right. "So you think that in spite of that prickly, cranky exterior of hers, I need to find a way to connect with her and give her another chance."

Roz nodded. "Believe me, I understand your hesitation. Frankly, I'd feel the same way. But I've been thinking about this. And I've learned enough from you to know that before you can even start with the actual polishing procedure, you have to spend time sanding the wood until there are no loose wood fibers on the surface. And you have to work using progressively finer grits of sandpaper. When Marge comes in the next time, use it as an opportunity to get to know her better. Because I also know that there has to be some underlying reason Marge pushes people away, and I don't believe it's just because her goal in life is to make people miserable." Roz caught Sadie's gaze. "Dig a little deeper and see if you can find a way past the woman's wall."

Sadie frowned, still not sure she wanted to take her friend's advice, as practical as it sounded.

"It's a lot like this bedroom set of hers," Roz went on. "In order to achieve the final beautiful finish, you have to go through hours of sanding and polishing in a process that isn't easy."

Sadie laughed. "Well, I can promise you that finding something in common with Marge isn't going to be easy either."

"No, it's not." Roz smiled. "But just like with every restoration project you take on, you might be surprised at what you find underneath."

17

SADIE SCRUBBED HER HANDS IN THE SMALL UTILITY SINK THE NEXT day, making sure she washed away the cleaning solution she'd used on the bedroom set. After drying her hands on a small towel, she took a bottle of water from the refrigerator in the corner of the Antique Mine's back room and stepped into the small fenced yard behind the store. Slowly, she began rotating her shoulders and stretching her back muscles. While Roz had been right about the difficulty of the project—and the difficulty of working with Marge—she still found herself enjoying the process. Taking something that many would simply scrap and finding the beauty in it was a labor of love.

She made a quick call to Edwin to see how his day was going and tell him about her progress with Marge's bedroom set. After they'd disconnected, she took a long drink of the water in the warm afternoon sunshine. She rolled her head gently in a circular movement. In a few more weeks, or perhaps even days, the daytime temperatures would drop considerably while the weather became intermittently dry and snowy. Mountain peaks surrounding Silver Peak would be blanketed in gleaming white, but for now, she was enjoying the sunshine warming the crisp air and the brilliant colors of the aspen trees in contrast with the deep hues of the evergreens.

The bell on the front door jingled. A moment later, Julie joined her outside in the sunshine.

"I thought you'd like to know I just helped the sweetest customers," Julie said with a grin. "Two sisters from Denver bought that old patent filing cabinet you picked up last month. Their father used to work in a patent office, and they plan to give it to him as a gift. They were absolutely thrilled about it."

Sadie took another sip of her water, then smiled. "You know how happy I am when someone connects personally to something in the shop."

Not only was the chest of drawers a wonderful piece, each drawer had been filled with logs of people who had filed patents, including the dates of the patents and their descriptions.

"What about you?" Julie asked. "How's the dresser coming along?"

"I was just telling Edwin about it." Sadie twisted the lid back on her water. "I think I might actually make Marge's deadline. Of course, I might have to pull a couple more late nights in the meantime, but I'm getting close."

"Every time I take a peek, it looks better and better. I know Marge will be so excited."

"I hope so." Sadie frowned, not as sure about that as Julie was. Again, she found herself wishing she didn't allow Marge to get under her skin as she did.

"Are you finished for the morning?" Julie asked.

"No, but I thought I'd take a short break before taking a few minutes to sort through that box of books Ashley brought me.

I told her I'd be happy to sell them on commission, but I need to make an inventory and verify the value of each of the books. With the week turning out to be so busy, I haven't had a chance to go through them yet."

"I'm happy to help until the next customer comes in," Julie offered.

"Perfect."

Julie carried the box of books from the storeroom into the back of the store and set it on a sturdy table.

"I can already think of a couple of customers who are always on the lookout for old and rare books," Sadie said, picking up the first volume. "And who knows? Maybe one of them will grab up the entire lot."

Sadie and Julie settled into the familiar routine they'd followed together dozens of times, cataloging all of the relevant information for each book such as author, title, publisher, copyright date, and condition.

Sadie picked up the next book on the top of the stack: *All about Railways: A Book for Boys* by F. S. Hartnell. A yellowed photo slipped out of the pages and slid onto the floor beside her.

"What's that?" Julie asked.

"Looks like an old photo." Sadie grabbed the photo and held it up under the light. "When Ashley brought the books over to me, she told me she'd found some photos that had belonged to her grandfather. But apparently she missed this one."

Julie leaned forward to see it. "Looks like quite a party."

Sadie studied the photo. Half a dozen men stood, holding up drink glasses and smiling. A sign on the wall above them said Silver Peak Drug Co. But it wasn't the men or even the sign that caught her attention. It was something in the background of the photo that drew her eye. A man, carrying a box filled with what appeared to be whiskey bottles like the ones Ashley had brought her, was walking through a door in the wall.

Sadie tapped her finger against the photo, then handed it to Julie. "This had to have been taken right next door. It used to be Silver Peak Drug Company before the Putnam family bought it."

Julie cocked her head and stared at the photo. "Makes sense, but I don't recognize that door."

"I don't either." Sadie flipped over the photo to look at the back. It had been inscribed *L. Solomon, 1922.* "Interesting. This was taken during the Prohibition era."

"Doesn't look to me like the place is alcohol-free."

"Definitely not, though it's no secret that during Prohibition people found plenty of ways to get around that law by making their own brew and holding their own parties. And a lot of 'medicinal' liquors were sold at the local drugstore. Either way," Sadie said, "Ashley will want this photo. L. Solomon must be Louis Solomon. Her great-great-grandfather."

"The same Louis who carved the missing chess set?"

Sadie nodded. "Exactly."

Sadie grabbed her smartphone from the counter, then tapped the screen to call the number she'd saved in her phone in case she needed to contact Ashley. She was still puzzling about the extra door as the phone rang. "No answer."

Ashley would want the photo, but in the meantime, the discovery brought up a number of other interesting questions in Sadie's mind. Ricky had mentioned that someone had been asking questions about the history of the hardware store. *Were they looking for something specific, or had they just been a tourist interested in Silver Peak's past?* Sadie wondered.

She and Julie went back to their task and finished cataloging the remainder of Ashley's old books. But long after they had finished, and Julie had returned to the counter to watch for customers, Sadie found herself staring at the photo, in particular at the man coming through the door, while sorting through the facts one by one in her mind. Decades ago, it seemed abundantly clear now, Putnam & Sons—or its building, at least—had been used by bootleggers. Bootleggers were known to use secret tunnels that linked their places of business to speakeasies. What if there were tunnels in town that had been used for that purpose, even under their very own Main Street?

The moment the thought entered her mind, Sadie shook away the possibility. The idea seemed absolutely ridiculous. But, on the other hand, in some sort of crazy way, it also made sense. Prohibition. Bootlegging. Speakeasies... And a mysterious ghost who'd left footprints at Putnam & Sons.

She couldn't believe it, but more she thought about it, the more it *did* make sense. There had been no sign of a break-in at Roscoe's shop, nothing on the surface that they had been able to discover. The video surveillance system Theo had set up had not revealed anyone coming in through the doors. Even the sheriff hadn't been able to determine where the intruder had come from.

As odd as it seemed, Sadie knew it was possible. Dozens of other towns across the country had tunnels beneath their streets. They'd been used for a number of things over the years, such as the smuggling of goods, even humans, during the Civil War. And sometimes they serviced less mysterious, more utilitarian purposes, such as being the conduits for steam vents or natural gas pipes.

But here in Silver Peak? How had no one known about it?

That was the question she kept coming back to over and over.

Sadie tapped the photo against her leg. No matter how she tried to look at things, the idea still seemed far-fetched. Four generations of her family had lived in Silver Peak. How could she not have ever even heard any rumors of tunnels beneath the city's Main Street? Surely her great-grandfather would have known about their existence, as well as Harry Polmiller's or Edwin's family. But Harry certainly had not mentioned it when she talked with him.

She pulled up the contact list in her phone a second time and connected to a familiar number.

"Hello again!" Edwin's voice resonated in the phone's small speaker next to her ear. "You must miss me this morning."

Sadie chuckled. "Well, yes, as a matter of fact I do. But I had a question, if you have a minute," Sadie said.

"Of course I do. What's up?"

"Well, this might sound crazy, but... Have you ever heard any rumors of tunnels being dug under Silver Peak? I mean, beyond the ones used for utilities, for example."

Edwin paused for a moment. "Well, no. And I doubt there's any official record of such things existing here in the town hall records. But it makes perfect sense, I suppose. After all, Silver Peak is a town built by people who dug tunnels for a living. And not everyone in town was necessarily an upstanding citizen." He laughed.

Sadie hadn't thought of it in those terms, but it certainly did make sense.

"I'm sure you're right—if people were digging and using tunnels for nefarious purposes, it's pretty unlikely they'd go get a permit from the city."

"Exactly," Edwin agreed. "I would more or less assume that any such tunnels were probably dug under the radar, official or otherwise. Are you thinking about Roscoe's store?"

"It certainly would explain our 'ghost's' mysterious comings and goings."

After they'd said their good-byes, Sadie stood there a few minutes more, contemplating the picture of the door in the wall. Where had it led? And what had happened to it?

18

"WHAT ARE YOU THINKING, SADIE?" JULIE ASKED, AND SADIE jumped as she realized she'd been lost in thought.

She hesitated before sharing her idea out loud. "What if there were secret tunnels under Silver Peak?"

"Secret tunnels?" Julie's brow furrowed. "Where did that thought come from?"

"I know it sounds kind of crazy, but it also would explain a lot. And Edwin seems to think it's possible too. We know now, because of those bottles, that there's a connection between the Browning House and Roscoe's store. Harry Polmiller remembers a couple of stories his parents talked about regarding the previous owners of Roscoe's building. They were believed to have been involved in both the local Mountain Mafia of Colorado and the bootlegging of alcohol during Prohibition. At the library, Roz and I also read how Louis Solomon was connected to the shooting of a deputy right here on Main Street that happened during a raid."

"Do you think that is related to the break-ins at Roscoe's store?"

"I realize it seems pretty far-fetched at this point, but what I do know is, strange things have been happening at both places.

And this door...if this is Roscoe's shop, the door isn't there now. Unless...unless it's hidden somehow."

Julie leaned forward. "So what's the plan now?"

Sadie's mind had yet to stop running though the possibilities. "Maybe if I can learn more about the Solomon family and the Browning House, I can figure out their connection to the Mountain Mafia. Maybe now I can even do some research on Prohibition-era tunnels."

"Makes sense to me."

Sadie went over to the mahogany desk where she kept her computer and sat down in a chair that, according to the dealer who sold it to her, had once belonged to Wyatt Earp.

"You have to admit that the twenties was an interesting time period," Sadie said as she typed *Louis Solomon* into the Google search box. "Did you know there were more pharmacists during this time period than there ever were before? Since whiskey could still be legally prescribed, medicinal alcohol sales increased substantially. And apparently orders for the amount of rubbing alcohol used for cleaning hospitals also increased dramatically as well."

"Sounds as if the Solomons knew how to make money," Julie said, hovering above her. She shuddered. "Though there must have also been a rise in the number of people dying from poisoning from tainted alcohol."

"I thought about that too." Sadie started reading through the options. "This could be him. *Hmm*...Well, there you go. The Solomons owned Silver Peak Drug Company." Somehow, at this point, Sadie wasn't surprised.

"Really?"

"And it looks like there's more. Louis Solomon and his brothers were arrested in connection to bootlegging alcohol during Prohibition. Here's what it says.

"Louis, Harry, and Robert Solomon—owners of Silver Peak Drug Co., in Silver Peak, Colorado, were arrested two nights ago after a search of their car by customs officers turned up outlawed liquor in their vehicle. The three brothers made no attempt to resist arrest and were taken to a local lockup facility, where they were photographed and fingerprinted. According to local law enforcement, a carload of commercial alcohol could bring in close to a million dollars. Which is why, when following the trail of revenue, thousands of law enforcement officers across the country continue to look the other way."

Sadie clicked back to the Google search page to see if she could find anything else, then stopped as a photo of a familiar face caught her eye halfway down the page. "And look at this. It's a photo of Adam Solomon."

"Ashley's uncle?"

Sadie nodded, then clicked on the photo. "Wait a minute… it's a mug shot."

"A mug shot?" Julie leaned in closer. "That's odd. What does it say about him?"

Sadie read the limited details out loud. "Adam R. Solomon, thirty-five years old, five feet, eleven inches tall, a hundred ninety-five pounds, was under arrest for five counts of fraud and one count of assault."

"That certainly puts a twist on the situation," Julie said. "Do you think he stole the chess set?"

"Honestly, I have no idea. But it does make me want to know what's actually going on. If he's running from the law, what's he doing here in Silver Peak?"

Fraud and assault? Something was clearly off. Adam had claimed he'd come to Silver Peak to help his niece.

Now Sadie wondered if his motive might be less altruistic.

19

WITH JULIE WATCHING THE STORE, SADIE HEADED OVER TO SEE Mac right away. She walked across the polished floors of the front lobby of the sheriff's office to the counter where the receptionist, Janet Parks, sat.

"Morning, Janet."

"How are you today, Sadie?"

Sadie smiled. "Great, thanks. How's your day going?"

"It was going pretty well until you showed up." Janet gave her a sly look. "Just kidding, of course! What can I do for you?"

As the undisputed queen bee of the sheriff's department, Janet was an unlikely combination of receptionist, administrator, and watchdog. While she seemed to relish the opportunity to spar with Sadie, making their interactions unpredictable, Sadie knew that the bluster was only a front for a good heart. Besides, Janet was a treasure trove of information—if she was in the mood to share it. But right now, Sadie needed to see Sheriff Slattery.

"I was wondering if the sheriff was available." Sadie glanced beyond the glass wall to where a couple of people stood talking. There was no sign of Mac.

"Do you have inside information on the ghost of Putnam & Sons?" Janet laughed.

Sadie chuckled. "Perhaps, though I'm pretty sure it's not a ghost."

"Considering he—or she—got into the store without any sign of entry…well, even you have to admit that's kind of odd." Janet picked up her phone and punched a button. "Let me see if the sheriff's out of his meeting yet."

A minute later, Janet waved Sadie to the back of the building, where the sheriff's office was located. The older man looked up from his desk, which seemed to be snowed under with paperwork.

"Morning, Sadie."

"Busy day?" Sadie asked.

Mac rested his elbows against his desk. "You could say that. Just returned from rescuing a couple of stranded motorists up the highway. The out-of-towners just don't know how to drive in these mountains."

Sadie nodded. "Any news on the thefts?"

"Unfortunately, no, but we've got every law officer in the state looking for the burglary ring. Janet's been spending most of her time fielding calls from people who are worried now that they've hit Silver Peak. And in the meantime, I'm just hoping we can track down these guys before they strike again."

"Well, I have some interesting information I think you need to know, though I have no idea if it's connected with the thefts." Sadie sat down across from the sheriff and told him both her theory on the tunnels between the town and what she'd discovered about Adam Solomon. "He's staying here in Silver Peak, Mac."

"Do you know where?" Mac asked.

"He's at the Crestview with his niece while they work on getting the Browning House ready to sell."

Mac flipped open his laptop and did his own search.

"I've never heard of any tunnels under Silver Peak, but you're right about Adam." Mac stood up and grabbed his jacket from behind his chair. "There's a warrant out for his arrest in connection with a whole slew of things. Fraud, burglary, assault..."

"What are you going to do?" Sadie asked, following the sheriff out of the room.

"I'm going to go find this guy. Because while it could just be a coincidence, I can't help but wonder if there might be a connection between him and some of the strange things that have been going on in town."

Thirty minutes later Sadie was at Putnam & Sons. She stood beside Roz and Roscoe in the back corner, showing them the photo she'd found and telling them her theory.

"A tunnel. Leading from my store." Roscoe shook his head. "I just don't see how it's possible. My family has owned this place for decades. It's been remodeled, repainted, refurbished... If there was some secret door leading to tunnels beneath Main Street, surely someone would have found it by now."

"And even if we've somehow missed discovering this hidden door," Roz said, "do you really think the residents of this town could keep something like that a secret for all these years? Just imagine what would happen if the *Chatterbox* gets wind of this idea. Whoever writes it would have a heyday with gossip about secret underground passages and a ghost running around Putnam & Sons."

Sadie laughed. "As crazy as it sounds, this photo is pretty strong evidence, if you ask me. And it gives us the only answer that explains how someone could walk into this store without going through the front door. It also explains the missing footage in Theo's video surveillance—because there was no missing video. They never came through the door."

"Sadie . . ."

"Just think about it. We know now that the previous owners of this building—the Solomons—were involved in bootlegging. And we know that the Browning House was used as a speakeasy during Prohibition."

Roscoe frowned, still looking not completely convinced. "Have you ever heard anyone mention any tunnels under Silver Peak?"

"No, but this would have been decades ago, and it wasn't something that was broadcast around town. Those involved would have known, but they would have done their best to keep it quiet. Especially if these tunnels were built in connection with the bootlegging of alcohol."

"I don't know." Roscoe glanced at Roz, who stood beside Sadie with her arms folded across her chest. "Don't tell me you're buying into this crazy idea."

Roz shrugged, hesitant. "I don't know, Roscoe. It's a logical possibility. And that photo . . ."

"It's not logical at all, as far as I'm concerned. And if it is true, where would we even begin to start looking?" Roscoe asked.

"I would assume that if there was some secret door to a tunnel, whoever built it in the first place would have made it hard to find." Sadie glanced at the spot where they'd set up the surveillance camera. "And the video recording will help. We watched the footage and know what parts of the store the thief didn't enter."

"True," Roz said. "That means we can eliminate the camera's line of sight, which includes the front of this wall, and we can at least narrow it down to where it definitely isn't."

"So the door would have to be somewhere along this large brick wall," Sadie said. She paused as a thought struck her. "The one wall you share with the Antique Mine."

"Or it could possibly be behind one of these wooden panels," Roz added. "You have the door to Arbuckle's on the other side of your store, Sadie. There could be a narrow passageway between the two stores."

"It's definitely possible," Sadie agreed.

"Okay." Roscoe shook his head. "I guess it's logical. And possible. But it's odd that either I or one of the other Putnams wouldn't have found it by now. Or mentioned it."

Someone had just come into the hardware store, and Roscoe glanced back to the front door.

"You go ahead, Roscoe, and help your customer," Roz said. "Sadie and I will look for the door."

Sadie watched Roscoe return to the counter, where he started ringing up a sale.

She slowly ran her fingers up the wall in one section, hoping none of Roscoe's customers needed to look at any merchandise where they were standing.

Roz glanced toward the front of the store, then turned to watch Sadie. "Personally, I hope you're right about all of this, because at least it would help explain what's been going on. Roscoe's just feeling, well, vulnerable over the recent thefts. Then there's your discovery at the library regarding the shady past of this property, and now this..."

Sadie kept searching the wall. If there was a door, one thing was certain. It wasn't going to be obvious. "What exactly did he say?"

"He finds the idea disturbing that this store had once been used to sell bootlegged alcohol. At least his own family wasn't involved. Or at least that's what we believe."

Sadie stopped to face Roz. "I remember meeting Roscoe's grandmother years ago. I have a feeling she was firmly on the side of those who supported Prohibition."

Roz laughed. "She was quite a woman. She never hesitated in speaking her mind. In fact, she had a lot to do in running Putnam & Sons all those years ago. She kept the inventory and books straight..."

"And she probably ensured everyone stayed sober at the same time."

Roz laughed. "If you are right, though, what exactly are we looking for?"

"A false wall, maybe a hollow sound when we tap? I'm sure whoever made it took great pains to keep it hidden." She stopped in front of a display of batteries and tapped on the wall behind it. Nothing.

If there was a tunnel here, they were no closer to finding it than they had been when she arrived.

20

SADIE DUG THROUGH THE BOX OF DRAWER PULLS SHE KEPT IN the back room, wishing there was something she could do with the information she'd just handed over to the sheriff about Adam. Hoping she'd been able to find the door in the photo, but all she really could do at this point was wait. She'd tried to call Ashley in the meantime, but there had been no answer. That had her worried. Was it possible the girl was involved in her uncle's illegal activities? Or was she completely ignorant of the fact her uncle was wanted by the authorities?

Ashley had told Sadie that her mother left Colorado when she was young, but Sadie didn't know why. All Sadie really knew at this point was that Adam Solomon wasn't the helpful uncle he claimed to be. And that more than likely the end of the Mountain Mafia hadn't signaled the end of the Solomon family's criminal involvement.

She pulled out a walnut tear drawer pull with an antique hand finish and held it up to the dresser. Many of the original drawer pieces on Marge's set either had been broken or were missing, which meant she was going to have to replace all of them. Her best bet was to wait for Marge to show up and see which style she liked the best, though Sadie would suggest the round hardwood knobs she'd bought at an estate sale last year. She had six of them that matched the dresser's wood perfectly, and the pewter inlay, with an intricate French Renaissance design, complemented the style of the bedroom set. She hoped Marge would agree.

She put the box of knobs aside, then turned back to the left side of the dresser. She loved this part of the restoration process: the moment when the years of damage and wear had finally been completely sanded away, and the new finish was complete, allowing the colors of the wood to shine in their original beauty.

Sadie had also taken Jean-Pierre's advice to rub out the shellac finish, a final step that many restorers chose to skip. But Sadie saw the wisdom in his guidance. She loaded a pad of steel wool with a paste wax she'd picked up at Putnam & Sons and started rubbing at the corner of the wood, making sure she went with the grain. The wax, Jean-Pierre had assured her, would act as a lubricant to help ensure a more consistent surface than if she'd decided to use a dry steel wool.

She continued rubbing in long, straight lines, careful to make sure that the scratch pattern left by the steel wool was uniform. The rubbed gloss was already beginning to look like she wanted it to, with a perfectly flat surface and no visible scratches. Waiting a week or more would have been better, but given Marge's tight time schedule, Sadie had decided to go ahead and start the process.

Finally finished with the dresser's side, Sadie took a step back to look at her work. As a restorer, she loved seeing the possibility in a piece; it was worth it to find the patience to take the time to transform it into its hidden potential.

The thought made Sadie pause as she began wiping off the wax with a paper shop towel before it dried. She glanced at the clock, Roz's words regarding Marge still fresh in her mind. Marge would be here soon, and she needed to find a way to connect with the woman. But talking to Marge was the last thing she felt like doing at the moment.

The store's bell jingled, and a minute later Marge stood in the doorway of the back room, her face flushed and the hem of her dress slightly askew.

"Morning, Marge," Sadie said, looking up from her work.

"Sadie."

Sadie finished wiping down the last corner where she was working, then took a step backward. "I'm on the final rub-down step. You can already see how it's really added to the beauty of the wood."

Sadie held her breath, bracing for Marge's reply. But it occurred to her that, no matter what the woman said, Sadie was thrilled with the outcome. The days of applying the shellac had resulted in the high-gloss finish she'd been hoping for, the finish that brought out the rich color of the wood grain, something no other finish could duplicate.

Marge stopped in front of the dresser, and Sadie heard her draw in a quick breath. "I have to say I'm quite surprised. It's . . . nice."

Nice? Coming from Marge, Sadie laughed to herself, it was the very zenith of praise. She studied Marge's face. "Marge . . . is everything all right? You look . . . flushed."

Marge ran her fingers across the top of the dresser. "I'm fine, it's just been a hectic morning. I'm worried about getting everything ready for when my family arrives. You will be done, won't you?"

"Of course." Sadie answered the woman's question, but her mind was on Edwin and Roz's advice that kept replaying over and over in her thoughts.

Sometimes taking the first step is actually the best way to soften a hard heart.

Try to find a way to build a rapport with Marge.

Find something the two of you have in common.

But how was she supposed to forgive *and* build a rapport with someone when they didn't seem to have anything in common at all?

"I do need your advice on something," Sadie finally said, grabbing the box of handles and setting them on the table, still unsure of what exactly to say. "The drawer pulls for the dresser all need to be replaced. I thought the round ones here would be the best match."

Marge took the knob offered to her and held it in her hand.

"What do you think?" Sadie asked. "I could find some online to order, but that could end up taking weeks, and we have these here right now."

"These are fine…"

"Because if you'd rather have a different color or style…" Sadie's voice tapered off.

Marge handed the knob back to her. "No, really. I think this one will look fine with the dresser."

"Great, because I have just enough of these on hand."

Sadie hesitated again. She'd expected Marge to storm into the shop impatiently, but instead she seemed…distracted.

"Listen, Marge. About the other day," Sadie began, both swallowing her pride and wondering how the woman was going to respond to an apology, "I am sorry for my sharp response. I know you've been under a lot of stress with your family coming into town."

Marge pressed her lips together and fiddled with the strap of her bulky purse while the familiar strains of Johnny Cash played in the background, cutting through the awkward silence.

Sadie thought back to each painstaking step she'd taken in restoring the bedroom set. Each step built on the one before it, and with each step, she'd seen the beauty of the antique furniture begin to emerge until it finally reached the rich patina that graced it now. Could the same thing happen in her relationship with Marge? All she could do was take the first step, even if it turned out to be only the first of many.

Marge turned away, but not before Sadie caught the internal conflict clearly expressed on the other woman's face. They might not ever become best friends, but trying to understand better where the woman was coming from couldn't hurt—along with extending a measure of grace even if the woman was responsible for a few dozen of Sadie's gray hairs.

"Johnny Cash has always been one of my favorite singers."

Sadie opened her mouth to reply. Where had *that* come from? Whatever she might have expected Marge to say, it wasn't that.

"Me too," Sadie said, surprised at where they'd found a connection. "I've always loved the old-time country music. Johnny Cash, Gene Autry, Loretta Lynn, Kitty Wells, Hank Williams..."

A wistful smile settled on Marge's face. "I went to one of Loretta Lynn's concerts back in the sixties. It pretty much cemented my love of country music. If I wasn't a fan before, I sure was after."

Sadie waited for Marge to continue, still surprised that their *something in common* had turned out to be a mutual love for country music.

Marge leaned forward, glancing around the store as if to be sure no one else might overhear. Apparently the time for confessions wasn't over yet. "You might find this hard to believe, but years and years ago, I dropped out of college to be the lead singer in a country band."

Sadie worked to mask the look of surprise on her face. She nodded in encouragement. "I had no idea you were once in a band. Sounds like a lot of fun."

"It was. We never made it to the billboard charts, but we were able to book enough gigs to keep steady work. Mainly county fairs, parks, and coffeehouses. We used to play a few original songs along with all the favorites. Johnny Cash... Patsy Cline... Hank Williams."

"Your family must have been proud of you."

Marge's smile faded, and she stiffened. "Becoming an entertainer didn't exactly fit with their plans for me."

"What were their plans for you?" Sadie asked, still trying to link Marge and the word *gigs* in the same thought.

"School. And then marriage to the right boy."

Sadie leaned back in her chair, realizing that this was the first lengthy conversation—one that went beyond the weather, the latest news on the *Chatterbox*, or even the ministries of Campfire Chapel—that the two of them had ever had. Clearly there was pain somewhere in Marge's story. Something had made her walk away from her music and settle with Lanford in Silver Peak. "What happened?"

"Billy, our band leader, was diagnosed with cancer, and the band ended up breaking up. I floated around for the next couple of years, with no real focus on what to do with my life. Eventually I met Lanford, married him, and moved with him here. Though I've always wondered what might have happened if I'd decided to stick to that career."

Sadie worked to process the news Marge had just given her. Peeling back the layers of Marge had certainly revealed more than Sadie had ever expected.

"Of course, even though I left the music business, and even though I married Lanford...the right sort of man...Well, I'm still the black sheep of the family," Marge continued, tapping her bright pink acrylic nails on the table. "My sister, for example, did everything my parents expected: married the right man, chose the right career path, and gave them the perfect grandchildren to carry on the family traditions. Millie and Max both went to Duke and graduated at the top of their classes."

"What happened to Billy?" Sadie asked.

"His cancer went into remission and he went back on the road. He found another lead singer and continued his career. We kept in touch." Marge's gaze dropped and she swallowed. "He...Billy...died last week unexpectedly. His wife called me and told me the news."

Now it was all coming together. Marge's stress, not just recently but as long as Sadie had known her. Lost dreams. Family expectations.

"Oh, Marge, I'm so sorry."

"Me too. His death has managed to stir up so many memories. Memories I'd tried so hard to bury over the years. I have a good life with Lanford, and I've never had any regrets over marrying him, but now... You must think I'm silly."

"No. Not at all." Sadie found herself barely breathing, for fear that Marge didn't suddenly come to her senses and regret pouring out her feelings in front of her.

"It's just that whenever I hear something—like Johnny Cash playing in the background—it reminds me of who I used to be. And who I ended up becoming. I suppose it's one of the things that always pulls me into your shop. And now...and now my family's coming at the end of the week, and all they are going to think about is how successful I could have been if I'd only married better and finished my degree."

Sadie shook her head. "Certainly, despite your not following their wishes, they loved you then and they still love you now. Too much time has passed for any of you to let it stand in the way of your relationship."

Marge's eyes darkened. "You don't know them."

For the first time, Sadie was able to look at the woman sitting across from her in a completely different light. She'd always seen Marge as brash and even irritating. And she was. But Sadie had never actually stopped to see what might be at the root of the woman's irritable disposition.

"I suppose I'm the one who should apologize. I've let my family's upcoming visit turn me into a nervous wreck. You didn't deserve the comments I made to you about your skills or your expertise."

"Marge..." Sadie stepped forward to hug the woman, but Marge abruptly turned away. She begin rifling through her purse, and then pulled out her keys.

"I'm sorry. I'm not sure what came over me." She straightened, pulling her shoulders back and her chin up, then pressed her purse against her side and marched toward the door. Clearly whatever had just passed between them was over. She turned as she exited the Antique Mine. "Lanford will be in touch to arrange a time for him to pick up the set."

21

An hour later, looking for a quick bite of lunch, Sadie and Roz walked into Arbuckle's, the small coffee shop housed in the old brick building next door to the Antique Mine. Sadie had always loved the cozy shop with its comfy, overstuffed chairs, and colorful throw rugs that added warmth to the shop. A woodstove stood in one corner while the delightful aroma of coffee beans permeated the air.

"You were right," Sadie said as she sat down on a padded armchair with one of Luz Vidal's savory muffins—spinach and artichoke—and a steaming mug of hot coffee.

"I was?" Roz took a sip of her coffee, clearly confused. "About what?"

"I finally tried doing what you suggested with Marge." Sadie lowered her voice, thankful the shop wasn't crowded. "Tried to find something—anything—we might have in common."

"And it worked?"

Sadie nodded. "I think so. At least for a time."

"Wow. I'm not sure I know how to respond to that." Roz sneezed twice, said "Excuse me," then pulled the paper off her muffin—jalapeño and cheddar—and took a bite.

"You really are coming down with something, aren't you?" Sadie asked, noticing her friend's eyes were watering and her nose was red.

Roz sneezed again, then nodded. "You're the one who told me something was going around. I probably should have settled for some herbal tea. But tell me about Marge."

"I don't want to say too much," Sadie said, not wanting to gossip, even with her best friend. "She went right back to her prickly self after we talked, but in the end I think I have a greater understanding of her."

"Well, I'm impressed."

"It wasn't me," Sadie said. "She's the one who found our commonality. And I wish I could tell you more about it, but I feel like I'd be betraying a confidence."

Roz's phone rang and she glanced at the caller ID.

"It's the sheriff," Roz said, setting down her coffee.

Sadie took a bite of her muffin while Roz took the call. A minute later, she hung up, then caught Sadie's gaze.

"You're not going to believe this," Roz said, "but Mac just found the chess set in the hotel room where Adam Solomon is staying."

At this point, Sadie wasn't surprised. "Did they find Adam?"

"No. Not yet. But the sheriff has asked both Roscoe and me to come down to the station immediately." Roz hesitated. "You'll come with me, won't you?"

"Of course."

A minute later, Sadie and Roz were headed down Main Street toward the sheriff's office. Sadie glanced at her friend as they crossed the street. Roz hadn't said another word about the sheriff's call since they left Arbuckle's. And that wasn't at all like Roz.

Sadie slowed down as they approached the sheriff's office. "You okay?"

"I'm not sure, to be honest." Roz waved her hands in front of her, as if she could simply dismiss the situation with the flutter of her hands. "All of this seems ridiculous because it is just a stolen chess set, but the whole situation is still... unsettling."

Sadie nodded, because she understood exactly what Roz was saying. "It really is."

Roz pressed her hand against her chest. "I'm so glad you think so too, because I was afraid it was just me overreacting."

"Not at all. It's not just a stolen chess set you're having to deal with," Sadie continued. "In the past week, you've found out that someone's been breaking in to your shop on a regular basis, and now it appears that the man responsible could very well be a wanted criminal."

"Well, when you put it that way, it definitely sounds unsettling." Roz let out a low chuckle. "Honestly, though, Sadie, all this makes me wonder what this world is coming to. I thought worrying about that group of thieves striking our town was bad enough, but this seems personal." Roz fiddled with the door handle but didn't immediately go in. "And why steal the chess set? It's all so strange."

"I think he might be looking for something other than a chess set."

"Do you really think there could be tunnels under Silver Peak that are hiding some kind of treasure?"

"I don't know, but I have a feeling Adam thinks so. The way I see it, it's the only thing I've been able to come up with that makes any kind of sense. If it's even possible to make sense out of all of this."

Roz shuddered beside her. "And now to think he's wanted by the authorities…"

"On the positive side, I have confidence in Mac. He knows what he's doing."

"I know." Roz looked up and caught Sadie's gaze.

A glance up at the two-story brick building that housed the sheriff's office brought Sadie back to the present and all of the questions that came with it. Roz was right, as far as she was concerned, that something strange was going on. And the sooner they found out the truth, the better.

She and Roz were just about to enter the sheriff's office, when Roscoe hurried toward them to catch up.

"Roz." Roscoe wrapped his arm around his wife's waist. "You okay?"

"Yes, and you?" she asked.

"To be honest, I'm simply grateful we know who's behind this. Maybe we can finally put an end to everything that's been going on."

"I agree, although I still have a lot of questions to ask. Because Adam had to have had a reason for stealing that chess set," Sadie said. "And knowing his past, I don't think it's purely sentimental. Let's hope Mac will have some answers."

The three of them stepped inside the lobby of the building, where Janet greeted them with a wry grin. "Sheriff Slattery is waiting for you. Looks like he might have caught your notorious ghost. You can go on back to his office."

"Thanks, Janet," Sadie said.

They met the sheriff inside his office. The now-familiar chess set sat in the middle of the wide, wooden desk in front of a large window overlooking the mountains. On any other day, Sadie would have stopped to take in the stunning view. Today, she was more interested in getting some answers.

"Roz... Sadie... Roscoe... thanks so much for coming by. I just need you to verify that this was the chess set you received for your birthday, Roscoe. And that it is the one that was stolen from the store."

"Yes." Roz nodded. "That's definitely it."

"It's a beauty, isn't it?" Roscoe added.

"Glad we found it. I was looking forward to stopping by Putnam & Sons on one of my days off and playing a game or two with you, Roscoe," Mac confessed.

"Maybe we'll get our chance after all. Now that it's back, anyway."

"I hope so."

"What about Adam?" Roz gripped the back of one of the chairs facing the sheriff's desk. "Did you find him yet?"

"No, we haven't been able to locate him. The desk clerk at the hotel told us he left yesterday afternoon, and she hasn't seen him since. With a warrant out for his arrest, a search warrant was easy to get. That's why we decided to search his room."

"Do you think Adam skipped town?" Sadie asked.

"I don't think so. All of his things were still there: his clothes, his shaving kit, and this chess set."

"Sounds like something spooked him," Roscoe said, glancing at Sadie. "Why else would he have left the chess set behind?"

"I have no idea. But I've updated the warrant that's currently out on him so all local and state law enforcement agencies will be on the lookout."

"What about Ashley?" Sadie asked. Regardless of what had happened to Adam, she was concerned for the girl. While Ashley still might be involved, Sadie's gut told her otherwise. "Have you spoken to her?"

"Not yet." Mac sat down behind his desk, then nodded for the three of them to sit down as well. "Kyle and I went by the Browning House a little while ago, hoping to find her there, but the place was empty. And she's not answering her phone. Kyle's waiting to see if one of them shows up."

"Do you think she's involved in this?" Roz asked.

"It's a possibility we can't ignore."

Sadie knew the sheriff was right. "I agree there's no way to know at this point if she's involved or not," Sadie said, still feeling the need to defend the young woman, "but when I spoke with her about the chess set, she seemed genuinely upset to learn it was missing. She was close with her grandfather as a child and was hoping to get it back."

"Which means she also had motivation to steal it," Mac said.

"True," Sadie acknowledged. "But I've been able to spend some time with her, and I don't think she's a part of this. And we know that not only was she in Denver for a job interview the night the chess set was stolen, she wasn't the one in the video Theo caught of our burglar."

"What I do know for a fact after looking him up on the police database is that Adam Solomon is wanted by the state authorities for a long list that includes credit card fraud, identity theft, and securities and commodities fraud."

"Do you think he's dangerous?" Roz asked.

"I certainly wouldn't put it past him. I even found one pending assault case against him." Mac shook his head. "The bottom line is that we'll have to wait to see if Ashley is involved in any of this, but there's no doubt Adam Solomon belongs behind bars. Apparently, he thought he could hide up here, but he's not getting away with this. Not if I have anything to do with it."

In the meantime, Sadie thought, they needed to find Ashley. Either she was involved and knew what her uncle was up to, or she was innocent. She replayed the conversations she'd had with the girl, trying to remember if there had been anything she'd missed, anything that might highlight the fact that Ashley—like her uncle—wasn't really who she said she was. Which was, in fact, the problem. If there had been any signs that the girl was a fraud, she'd missed them.

On top of that, Ashley had seemed to truly care about her grandfather and she appeared to regret the fact that she hadn't had the opportunity to get to know him better before he died. That tended to make Sadie believe the girl had no idea what the Solomon family had been involved in.

"Sadie?"

She glanced up at Roz. "Sorry, I was just thinking."

"About?" Roz prodded.

"My conversations with Ashley. I was trying to remember anything she said that might help us figure out where she might have gone."

"And?" Mac asked.

Sadie shook her head. "At the library she mentioned how much she enjoyed Silver Peak. How she grew up in a large city, so she appreciated the fact that we don't have any smog or traffic, and that people actually said hello to each other."

"What else?" Mac asked.

Sadie ran through the rest of the conversations in her mind, trying to pair the words with what Ashley might be feeling right now. According to the sheriff, the desk clerk at the motel hadn't seen Adam since the day before. It was possible that he'd returned to Pueblo for the day to work—as Sadie knew he'd done before—still clueless of what the lawman had found out. Or maybe he'd gotten wind that they were looking for him and he'd gone into hiding. There was a chance that Ashley had seen the sheriff pull up to the Browning House, and that she was still there, scared and alone.

A sudden thought came to Sadie. She looked up and caught Mac's gaze. "I think I might know where we can find Ashley."

22

"WAIT A MINUTE." THE SHERIFF FOLDED HIS ARMS ACROSS HIS chest and leaned back against his chair. "You think you know where she is?"

"It's a long shot," Sadie admitted, "but if she isn't working at the Browning House or at the hotel, I think she might be in Centennial Park."

"Why Centennial Park?" Mac asked, doubt still clear on his face.

"When I talked to her at the library last week, she told me it was a place she liked to go to be able to think. You said that Adam has been gone since yesterday afternoon," Sadie continued. "If she's innocent, she might not even know where he is. Which means she might not be able to get ahold of him. And she might be scared."

"That's all possible," Roscoe said, "but I don't think we have enough information to even make that judgment."

"I agree." Mac nodded. "But I still think it's worth checking out." He stood up and grabbed his keys. "I'll head over to the park now..."

"Wait..." Sadie hesitated. Her gut might be telling her that Ashley Solomon was innocent, but she was afraid the girl still might run if she saw the sheriff coming. "Let me go by myself. She and I have connected over the past week, and I think she might be honest with me. That is, if she knows anything."

Mac glanced at his watch. "I'll give you twenty minutes. If I haven't heard from you by then, I'm sending out a search party to find you."

Sadie shot him a smile. "Okay."

"You're sure about this?" Roz asked.

"Positive."

As Sadie left the sheriff's office, she stopped and redialed Edwin's number. When he answered, she explained what was happening.

"Do you need me there with you?" he asked, sounding concerned.

"No, but thanks. I suspect Ashley will respond better if I'm by myself. I really don't think she has anything to do with the break-ins or the chess set."

"You know I'll be there in a heartbeat if you need me."

"I know, and I appreciate that more than you can know. But I'll be fine. Mac is aware of what's going on, and so are Roz and Roscoe."

"Keep me posted."

"Will do."

She headed down Jefferson Avenue toward Water Street, where Centennial Park was located on the edge of Silver Peak. Just as she'd hoped, Ashley was sitting on one of the bandstand bleachers that was used for concerts. She was wearing a pair of gray sweatpants and a pink sweatshirt.

Sadie sent up a quiet prayer for wisdom and the right words.

"Hi, Sadie." Ashley smiled up at her when she saw her approach. "It's good to see you. Out for a walk?"

"Actually, I'm here to see you. I remember you told me how much you loved this place. Would you mind a little company?" Sadie asked.

"Of course not. I was just enjoying the cool air and the sunshine." Ashley tucked a strand of hair behind her ear. "What's up?"

Sadie hesitated, but she knew she needed to go ahead and tell Ashley why she was there. She took a deep breath. "There's something I need to talk to you about."

"That sounds serious. What's wrong?" Ashley looked up at her, squinting in the afternoon sun. Sadie was feeling more and more certain that Ashley didn't know what was going on with her uncle.

"The sheriff found your grandfather's chess set."

"He did? That's fantastic! Where was it?"

Sadie's fingers gripped the edge of the bleacher where she sat. Either Ashley was a very good actress or she was telling the truth.

"In your uncle's hotel room."

Ashley's smile faded immediately. "I don't understand. His hotel room? Why would he... How did he...?"

"Ashley... Your uncle's wanted by the authorities on a number of serious charges."

"What? No..." She shook her head and stood up. "I don't know who told you that, but they're wrong, Sadie. He came here to help me. He's family. The family my mother took me away from."

Sadie caught the hurt in her voice and wished desperately the truth had turned out to be something different. "Ashley, do you know why your mother left Colorado?"

The young woman's gaze dropped as she sat back down beside Sadie. "She never would tell me. She just walked away and took me with her."

"I know it's hard for you to hear this, but I've just come from the sheriff's office. Your uncle's involved in a number of illegal activities, including fraud and assault."

"And my grandfather? Was he involved as well?"

"There are connections between the Solomon family and a local mafia. They've disbanded now, but..."

"That must be why my mother left."

"It's possible."

Ashley stared out across the park, clearly trying to absorb the information Sadie had just given her. "The sheriff... He thinks I'm involved as well, doesn't he?"

"There is some evidence that points to your innocence," Sadie said, speaking of the video, "but he's going to want to ask you some questions."

Ashley blew out a deep sigh. "I knew this house was going to bring me nothing but trouble. All I want to do is leave and put all this behind me."

"You lost your grandfather." Sadie rested her hand lightly on the younger woman's arm. "That's not something you can just put behind you so easily."

Ashley shrugged. "My mother did. She just walked away. Maybe she was right. I never should have come here."

"I'm so sorry things haven't turned out the way you'd hoped."

Ashley turned and caught Sadie's gaze. She seemed confused and blindsided. "Will you stay with me? When I go talk to the sheriff?"

"Of course. You know I'll do anything I can to help."

Sadie took a seat beside Ashley in Mac's office, not sure if she was supposed to defend the girl or simply sit and listen. A lawyer she was not. Of course, Edwin was one, but she felt sure that all Ashley needed right now was a friend... and she could easily be that. The sheriff leaned against his desk, his arms folded across his chest, his face stern.

"When's the last time you saw your uncle?"

Ashley fumbled with her purse as she set it on the floor beside her, her gaze fixed on the chess set still sitting in the middle of the sheriff's desk. "I don't know... sometime yesterday afternoon. He told me he had some work he needed to get done and not to expect him for dinner. I grabbed something to eat in town, then went back and worked in the house till about ten last night."

"Did you speak with him at all?"

"No. I tried to call him when I got back to the hotel, but he didn't answer. I figured he'd gone to bed early."

"And you didn't see him this morning?"

"There was a note stuck under my door telling me to go ahead and leave without him because he was stuck doing some project. The note said he didn't want to wake me." Ashley looked to Sadie, her fingers gripping the edges of the table as she leaned forward. "I'm sorry. I still don't understand what any of this is about. Am I in trouble?"

"That depends. Did you know your uncle is wanted by the authorities?"

"Not until Sadie told me." Ashley's jaw tensed. The girl was clearly spooked. "Three weeks ago, I received a call from my grandfather's lawyer. He said that my grandpa had passed away and had left me a few things in his will, including the Browning

House. My uncle offered to come with me to Silver Peak and help me sort out my grandfather's property. He even offered to pay my travel expenses and hotel bill while I'm here."

"You mentioned that you hadn't seen your mother's family for a long time," Mac said, taking down a few notes on a pad of paper.

"My mother and I moved to Seattle when I was about nine. I haven't seen any of her family members since then—until now. But when I showed up for the funeral, they were all so nice to me. Treated me like family. Adam especially. Like I said, he offered to come help me figure out what to do with the house. He said we should put aside our differences because we were family." Ashley's fingers tightened around the hem of her sweatshirt. "I always wanted to believe that the rift between my mother and her family was just that. A rift. Some misunderstanding. Not because she was trying to protect me from something bad."

"What do you know about the Solomon family?" Mac asked.

Ashley looked up, her eyes rimmed with tears. "When I was little, I remember spending time with my grandfather. He was a master at puzzles. Coming here to Silver Peak reminded me how little I knew about him and my family history. I knew they had lived here for a while, and obviously owned the Browning House. I was curious to know more."

"Puzzles?" Mac asked.

"Primarily wooden ones, but he also loved riddles and brainteasers."

"Did he solve puzzles? Or…"

"He was always making them for me. You know, like wooden toys, but they were puzzles I had to solve."

"What about treasure hunts?" Sadie asked, speaking up for the first time.

Ashley nodded. "It sounds silly now, but that's why I thought leaving me the house and the chess set...even the books...were some kind of puzzle. Something he wanted me to figure out."

"But you didn't find anything?" Sadie asked.

"No. I guess I was just searching for something that I'll never find."

The sheriff folded his arms across his chest and leaned back against the desk. "You've admitted you had motivation to steal that chess set."

Ashley's eyes widened. "But I didn't. I didn't know where it was. And I have no idea why Adam took it. You have to believe me." Ashley turned to Sadie. "I told you, strange things were happening at the house. I don't want to believe Adam had anything to do with it, but what if it was him?"

"He had access to the house," Mac pointed out. "What reason would he have to sneak around?"

"What if he wanted the property?" Sadie suggested.

"Why would he want the property?" Ashley asked. "You've seen how run-down it is. It's going to cost more than it's worth just to fix it up."

"Then there has to be another reason," Sadie said. The tunnels? "You were reading a book on local treasure hunting at the library."

"Adam mentioned something one day about a lost cache of money his father had talked about once. When I questioned him further, he told me to forget it. That it was nothing. But it got me curious."

"What if Adam *was* looking for something, Mac. Maybe something he'd heard about in a store from his own father. That would mean there has to be a connection between the house and the chess set and the photo I found that suggests there could be a tunnel. It might even connect the Browning House to Putnam & Sons." Sadie turned back to Ashley. "Did your grandfather ever talk about the chess set holding a secret?"

"No, nothing I can remember. He did tell me stories about his grandfather, though, while we played."

"Do you remember any of them?"

"I was nine, and not really interested in family history at the time." Ashley let out a soft laugh. "I just remember that Louis Solomon's father came over on a boat in search of a better life back at the end of the eighteen hundreds. He ended up in Colorado searching for gold, and eventually found work in the silver mines. He didn't strike it rich, but he made enough money to buy the Browning House."

Mac smacked the desk with his hand. "What are we missing?"

"I almost forgot, but there is one other thing I found." Ashley drew in a deep breath and turned to Sadie. "Remember I told you I had found some old photos in the books."

"Yes."

"Well, I found something else. A letter, which I'm pretty sure was written by Louis."

"Can we see it?" Mac asked.

Ashley nodded, then opened her purse and pulled out the letter before handing the fragile paper to the sheriff.

Mac slid on his glasses, his brow furrowed as he read it to himself.

"What does it say?" Sadie asked, trying to curb her excitement.

Mac handed her the letter. Sadie clutched the thin, yellowed paper and started reading.

April 21, 1922

Dear R,

I fear the end of my life is near, my friend. An officer was killed two blocks from my house last night on Main Street, and I feel certain they will find a way to tie it back to me even though I wasn't involved. This morning, my brother was arrested and taken in for questioning, and while they were unable to prove he was involved, I've been told they are now searching for me.

For too long, I have justified the two lives I live; I thought I could rationalize my involvement in the illegal ventures of our association by giving to various charities and needy families in our community, but even that isn't enough anymore. Perhaps I'm simply getting too old, but as lucrative as our new business has been—helping to quench the thirst of this state—I fear for my family, and for the position I have put them in.

I have hidden the remaining balance I owe you—with an additional large bonus—in the usual. My debt is paid. But for me I fear my only option is to disappear. Please do not try to find me.

Sincerely,

L

"Louis Solomon," Sadie said, not even trying to hold back the surprise.

"I wonder how this letter ended up in an old pile of books," Mac asked.

"And where their 'usual hiding place' was." Sadie handed the letter back to Ashley. "You know, Roz and I read about something a few days ago at the library. It also mentioned an officer being killed during a standoff on Main Street, and that there was a large amount of cash purported to be missing, as well as twenty thousand dollars' worth of illegal spirits confiscated."

Ashley folded the letter and slipped it back into her purse. "Do you think that's what Adam is after?"

"It's very possible," Sadie said. "Wherever there was bootlegging, there was definitely money involved. This was how those guys became rich."

"Did Adam see this letter?" Mac asked.

"Of course," Ashley said. "I didn't think anything about it at the time. I thought he was helping me."

"It more than likely verified any stories he'd heard from his father," Sadie said.

Ashley glanced up at the sheriff, a look of sadness across her expression. "So what happens now?"

"Adam was looking for something." Sadie nodded toward the desk. "I think we need to find out what secret this chess set is holding."

23

THAT EVENING, SADIE SET THE CHESS SET ON ROZ'S DINING ROOM table, thrilled, like the rest of them, that the sheriff had found the board. She was equally grateful that after the sheriff had taken photos and finished his report, he'd allowed Roz to take it home until its ownership could be sorted out. Sadie was also certain Mac still wasn't a hundred percent convinced Ashley wasn't involved with the theft, but with no evidence to hold her, he'd let her go. And Sadie, ready to give her the benefit of the doubt, had ask Ashley to come with her to Roz's house. If anyone could give them insight into the Solomon family, Ashley could.

Edwin had joined them, eager to hear all about what had happened. Theo and Sara crowded around the table beside Sadie, Edwin, Roscoe, and Roz, clearly just as interested in what was going on.

"Wow, Grandma." Theo slid open the narrow drawer of the chess board and started pulling out the intricately carved pieces. "This really is beautiful."

"Beautiful and mysterious," Roscoe added, as Roz set down a tray of hot chocolate, coffee, and a plate of brownies next to the chess set.

"Do you remember anything your grandfather might have mentioned to you about this set, Ashley?" Sadie took one of the mugs of coffee and added a spoonful of sugar to it. "Anything that might help us figure out why your uncle would have wanted to steal it?"

"Trust me, I really wish I could help. Ever since I found out what Adam did, I've tried to think of something—anything—that might explain his actions, but I honestly don't know." She picked up the queen from the drawer, held it in front of her, and shrugged her shoulders. "Adam was pretty private about his work, but I never thought he might be involved in something illegal. I honestly thought he was here to help me."

"Then since we can't talk to Adam," Sadie said, taking a sip of her coffee, "we need to figure out why your grandfather willed this chess set to you. He had to have had a reason. And more than likely, it's the same reason Adam had for taking the set."

"But what exactly are we looking for?" Sara asked.

"That is the question we have to answer." Sadie had asked herself the same thing over and over, but so far, all the pieces were refusing to come together. "All we really know is that this chessboard holds some kind of secret. A secret Adam was willing to break the law for."

"We don't even really know that for sure," Edwin pointed out. "Though it seems like the most likely conclusion.

"*The Secret of the Old Chessboard*," Sadie said. "It sounds like a lost Nancy Drew novel."

Roz laughed as she took one of the mugs of coffee and sat down next to her husband.

"Do you think it could hold a treasure?" Roscoe asked. "That would be a pretty good reason to steal it, right there, if he thought so."

"Could be." Sadie nodded. "While doing some research in the library a couple of days ago, Roz and I came across evidence of a large amount of missing money right here in Silver Peak."

"According to an article we read," Roz explained, "back during Prohibition, three deputies raided one of the businesses on Main Street and found over twenty thousand dollars' worth of illegal spirits. There was also a large amount of cash purported to be missing from the premises."

"Who was involved?" Theo asked.

Sadie hesitated to answer the question, knowing how betrayed Ashley already must feel by the knowledge that her mother's family had hardly been upright citizens.

Ashley shook her head. "It's okay. Hiding the truth won't help anyone at this point."

Sadie nodded, knowing the young woman was right. Ashley's mother had tried to run away from the truth, and in the end all it had managed to do was hurt them all.

"Ashley's great-grandfather's name was mentioned as a suspect in the article, but at that time, the missing money hadn't been found yet. We don't even know for sure whether he was actually involved."

"I guess I shouldn't be surprised by any of this." Ashley's eyes glistened with tears. "I'm beginning to understand why my mother decided to cut ties with her family. I'd hoped that all the rumors of their shady activities would turn up to be false, but now..."

"There is something else." Sadie pulled out the yellowed photo she'd found in one of the books Ashley had given her out of her purse. "I found this yesterday. I tried to call you, but I couldn't get ahold of you."

"What is it?"

"I found a photo in one of your grandfather's books."

Ashley held up the photo. "Louis Solomon. 1922. He would have been...I guess in his midthirties at that time."

"The photo was taken in the local drugstore, which is now Putnam & Sons," Sadie added. "Your family used to own the building."

"And from the looks of what's going on in the photo," Ashley said, "I don't think there's any question that my family was involved in bootlegging."

Sadie reached out and squeezed Ashley's hand. "There's still a lot that we don't know, but none of it should stop you from holding on to the memories you have of your grandfather and family. Whatever the truth might turn up about your family's past, it's clear to me that your grandfather loved you deeply."

"I know." Ashley drew in a deep breath and nodded. "But what happens now? We have a possible lost treasure from bootleggers, a chess set clearly hiding its own secrets, and a number of strange things happening both at the hardware store and at the Browning House."

"I think there has to be something behind these inscriptions." Sadie ran her fingers across the side of the set. "Did your grandfather ever talk about them, Ashley?"

Ashley shook her head. "I don't remember talking about them, but it's been so many years. We played by the hour and talked about all kinds of things. I just remember him telling me that his grandfather had carved all of it by hand. The board and every one of the pieces."

Sadie stared at the board, wondering what she was missing. "Ashley, you told me that your grandfather made puzzles and that he learned how to do that from his grandfather."

"Yes..."

"And he made this chess set back in the 1920s, when he and his family were involved in bootlegging in the area," Sadie continued.

Edwin leaned forward. "Maybe there's some sort of hidden message."

A hidden message... Sadie mulled over Edwin's words.

"Wait a minute." Sadie set her coffee mug down, her mind still working through the pieces. "What if there's a clue *inside* the chessboard?"

"That would make sense," Roz said. "But where? There's a drawer, but the rest of it looks pretty solid."

"What if instead of words running together..." Sadie turned the board slowly in each direction. *Letters*... *numbers*... "What has both letters and numbers?"

"You think it's a puzzle?" Ashley asked.

"Some kind of code." Edwin added.

"If your grandfather—and his grandfather—loved puzzles, that would make sense," Roscoe said, sipping at his drink.

"What if they're chess moves?" Ashley threw out.

Sadie nodded at the suggestion. Maybe they were getting somewhere after all. "That makes sense to me too. So we look at the inscriptions as chess moves instead of words."

"And what if those chess moves open up a locked drawer?" Theo palmed his hands against the table. "I saw a video online once that showed you how to use magnets to open a secret drawer."

Sadie turned to her granddaughter, her excitement growing. "Do you have your phone with you?"

"Of course."

"Look up 'secret compartment in a chess set.' Maybe we can get some ideas of how Louis Solomon might have done this."

"Here we go...," Sara said a few moments later. "This is an example of a board with a secret drawer that stays locked unless the pieces are arranged properly."

"How does it work?" Roz asked.

"*Hmm...*" Sara scrolled down the page. "Theo was right. It looks like you can do it with magnets. Magnets on the bottom of the chess pieces...When the chess pieces are on the correct square, which has a switch, then the square slides open and a spring-loaded drawer pops out."

Sadie grabbed a queen off the board and walked across the room. She'd noticed that the pieces were heavy the first time she and Roz had played a game with them, but she'd figured it was because they were made from solid wood.

What are you trying to tell us, Louis Solomon?

Sadie pressed the bottom of the piece against the refrigerator.

It stuck.

Sara stepped up beside her and pulled it off. "It's magnetic."

"Which means there *has* to be a secret compartment," Theo said. "And while there isn't a lot of room, there could be enough space for a small drawer."

"But why?" Ashley asked. "What was he trying to hide?"

"You could hide anything small. Money... a map... a key."

"If you ask me," Roscoe said, folding his hands across his chest, "he could have just given you directions on how to open it up instead of all this cloak-and-dagger nonsense."

Ashley smiled. "You didn't know my grandpa. He wouldn't have thought that was nearly as much fun."

"We're looking for a pattern, then," Roz said, hovering over the board. "Which means you all might have been right about the inscriptions being chess moves."

"Grandpa taught me how to write them down as we played," Ashley said, "but that was so long ago, I don't think I can remember most of them."

"That's okay," Sadie said. "Why don't you Google 'chess moves,' Sara. How are they written?"

Sadie took another sip of coffee while she waited for Sara to find the right page, excitement beginning to brew inside her. If they could find what Louis Solomon had hidden inside the chessboard, they would be one step closer to discovering the truth of what had been happening at Putnam & Sons.

"Here we go. Really?" Sara looked up and frowned before reading from her phone's display. "To record and read chess moves, you can use algebraic notation." She rolled her eyes. "Ugh... math."

"Go on," Theo urged.

"Okay. In a serious tournament game, it looks like it's actually a rule that you write down every move." She scanned further down the page. "Basically, uppercase letters are used to identify every piece on the board, with the exception of the pawn. The letter used is the first letter in the name of that piece."

"So for example, *K* would be used for king, Q for queen, et cetera?" Sadie asked.

"Exactly."

"And for the pawn?" Theo asked.

"Um . . . no letter is used for the pawn."

"This all seems too complicated to me," Roz said, sitting back down at the table.

"Why don't you keep reading?" Sadie said.

"Okay." Sara scrolled down the screen. "On top of that, each of the sixty-four squares has a unique name. So when making a capture, you insert an *X* between the first letter of the piece, ending with the destination square."

"So, for example . . . ," Theo began. "*Qxe7* would mean that your queen captures a piece on e7."

"I think that's right," Sara said.

"There's a problem," Sadie said, studying the board. "I don't know about the rest of you, but the letters don't seem to work. For starters, I don't see any *K* or *Q*."

"I don't either," Roscoe said.

"Well, it was a good idea, anyway." Roz cupped her mug in her hands.

"Wait a minute," Sara said, still reading from her phone's small display. "What if you don't live in an English-speaking country?"

"What do you mean?" Ashley asked.

"Listen to this," she continued reading off her phone. "It says that German players, for example, use an *S*, which is short for *Springer* for the knight, and in French they use an *F*—short for *Fou*—for the bishop."

"Louis Solomon married a German woman," Ashley said, her eyes brightening.

"Maybe that's it." Sadie felt the rush of excitement return. "Roz, do you have a pad of paper and a pen?"

"Of course." She pulled a small pad of paper out of the kitchen drawer then handed them both to Sadie.

"All we have to do now is follow the moves," Sadie said, hoping it would end up being as simple as it sounded. "Theo, why don't you read the moves off to me, one at a time. Sara, we'll need the German names of the queen, the bishop, and so on."

"Got it."

They started slowly with Sadie calling out the moves from the inscriptions, Sara translating the moves into German, and Theo sliding the pieces across the board.

Five minutes later, a second drawer popped open.

"I can't believe it," Sadie said, smiling at her grandchildren. "We did it!"

"I think Ashley needs to do the honors," Roscoe said, looking as excited as Sadie felt as everyone stared at the open drawer. "Considering your great-great-grandfather is the one who carved this beauty, and your grandfather clearly wanted you to have it."

Ashley hesitated before pulling out what was in the drawer. "You're sure?"

"Definitely," Roz said. "Just don't keep us in suspense. What's in there?"

"It looks like a map...and a key." Ashley laid them both on the table.

Sadie picked up the map and unfolded it. "This looks like downtown Silver Peak." She handed the yellowed paper to Roscoe. "What do you think?"

"I think you're right, but something's off. For example, there shouldn't be a road here." Roscoe pointed to the center of the map.

Sadie took the map back to study it further, her heart racing. "I don't think they're trying to depict a road there. I think these are tunnels!"

"Sadie's right," Roz said. "And it looks as if there's a space between the two stores."

"I can't believe I'm saying this, Sadie," Roscoe said, going over the map for himself, "but I think you might have been right about the tunnels."

"Tunnels?" Sara shook her head. "So you *were* right, Grandma."

"What did you say?" Sadie quipped. "Could you repeat that?"

Everyone laughed, and Sadie continued. "There are old tunnels in Colorado Springs, for example. There's an old avenue there, lined with Victorian houses with tunnels that go from that respectable neighborhood to other, less than respectable locations. I have a feeling there are a lot of things that went on in this town that never made it into the history books. The boom that hit Silver Peak made a lot of people rich, but there definitely was a darker side."

"It still seems kind of crazy, though beyond cool as well," Sara said.

"I agree." Theo nodded, picking up the key. "But if there's a hidden door, how is it possible no one has found it? I mean, you'd think someone would have discovered it by now."

"I don't know," Roscoe said, "but it does explain how someone has been getting in and out of my store without getting caught."

"And how the video surveillance didn't pick up their coming and going," Theo added.

"You're both right." Sadie picked up the key.

Theo glanced at his watch, then frowned. "Mom wants us home by seven. Both of us still have homework that's due tomorrow."

"She won't mind if we stay out..."

"Sara," Sadie began.

She held up a hand in protest. "I know what you're going to say. I just don't want to miss any of this."

"I promise to let you know if we find out anything new. And in the meantime," Sadie said, "the rest of us can head over to the store and see if we can find out what this key goes to."

24

Roscoe, Sadie, and Edwin dropped off Theo and Sara at their house, after arranging to meet Mac at Putnam & Sons. With Roz's head cold growing worse, Ashley had offered to stay at the house with her and keep her company, but Sadie was pretty sure the girl had used that as an excuse not to run into her uncle. And really, Sadie couldn't blame her.

Although part of Sadie couldn't help but be excited over what they'd found in the chess set, another part of her was worried about what they might still discover.

Five minutes later, Sadie, Edwin, and Roscoe stood beside the sheriff in the middle of Putnam & Sons, staring at the wall of the hardware store. Nearly all the buildings in Silver Peak's business district were made of brick, including Roscoe's store, but according to the map they'd found, this one apparently had something extra leading away from it. A tunnel.

Sadie walked slowly down the far right aisle, studying the wall as she'd done earlier today for any inconsistencies in the brick and wood panels. If there was a door here, it clearly wasn't going to be easy to find. That fact that no one had stumbled across its existence over the past few decades was proof enough of that.

"We might have a key," Edwin said. "But we don't even know where to start."

"We do have this." Sadie unfolded the map they'd found in the chess set and set it down on the counter at the back of the store. It wasn't more than a rough sketch, but at least it narrowed the search down a bit. "You're right, though. I don't know how much it's going to help. According to the map, there's a small passageway between our two shops, and it looks like there are at least two tunnels between here and the Paseo River. But we still need to find where the door is."

Sadie walked back to the wall and ran her hand across the row of bricks above the built-in wooden drawers. "I think we were on the right track before. According to the map, it has to be in this general vicinity, or maybe even behind this section of drawers."

"Do you know when these were put in, Roscoe?" Mac asked, nodding at the drawers.

"From what I remember, my grandfather put them in after he bought the building. He loved the convenience of organizing small things with the drawers. But unless we're missing something, there doesn't seem to be a visible keyhole."

"Or signs of a door," Edwin pointed out.

"And here's another problem," Sadie added. "These drawers are built-in, but whoever's been accessing the store has clearly been going in and out."

"Which would make it impossible to do where they're built in," the sheriff said.

"Exactly." Sadie frowned. That potentially narrowed their options even further. But to where?

They divided the brick portion of the wall into a grid and assigned sections to each person. Sadie combed through hers inch by inch, square by square. Thirty minutes later no one had found anything.

Sadie took a step back, then started going over in her mind everything they knew about Louis Solomon. He'd been involved in a number of unscrupulous activities, including the bootlegging of alcohol and the running of a speakeasy in the Browning House. He was also said to have been a member of the Mountain Mafia—but he had one other important skill that couldn't be forgotten. Louis Solomon was also a master wood-carver.

"What if we're looking in the wrong place?" Sadie wondered out loud. "After all, Louis Solomon loved to carve wood and he was very good at it."

"So it might make sense that he would hide the tunnel behind the wooden panels," Edwin suggested, moving from the brick wall over to the large paneling.

"Look at the floor over here," Roscoe said. "It's faint, but there's a mark."

"They look like scratch marks," Sadie said. "Barely visible, but definitely there."

Sadie bent down beside them and ran her fingers across the marks. Maybe they were finally on the right track. "What do you know about these panels, Roscoe?"

"I'm fairly sure they were a part of the original architecture of the store," Roscoe said. "In fact, I've thought of taking them out in order to add more shelving, but Roz has always discouraged me."

Sadie ran her hand slowly across the intricately carved panels above the marked flooring.

"If you're right, this is crazy," Roscoe said, shaking his head. "To not have stumbled across this after all these years…it just seems impossible."

"Louis Solomon was clearly good at what he did," Sadie said, continuing to feel for anything out of place. "Hidden hardware and perfect lines matching the architecture of the store would help make it invisible."

Mac nodded as he searched beside her. "Barrel-style hinges would do the trick as well."

Sadie pushed on a small section of the carved panel. And then—something clicked. Damp, musty air greeted them as the door creaked open.

"This is crazy." Roscoe stared at the opening beside Sadie. "All these years, there's been a secret passage into our store."

"Anyone game for going in?" Sadie asked.

"Definitely, but if we're going to go in there, we'll need these." Roscoe handed each of them flashlights from one of the shelves.

Mac Slattery shone his flashlight into the tunnel, revealing a row of narrow steps that disappeared down into a dark passageway. "This might explain why your burglar was stealing flashlights and batteries."

Edwin chuckled. "He wasn't after your money, Roscoe. He was after your supplies."

They stepped into the dark tunnel, single file, with the sheriff in front, then Sadie and Edwin, and Roscoe bringing up the rear. Sadie flipped on her flashlight. The beam of light picked up the cold stone and faint tracks of mud on the tunnel floor.

"*Brr*...it's chilly in here." Sadie hesitated for a moment in the doorway. "I also have a feeling that there are going to be a few critters who have taken up residence in here."

Sadie shivered as her flashlight caught a spider in its beam, casting its huge shadow along the wall. Cobwebs hung from the low ceiling, causing her to duck. No more than four feet wide and just over six feet tall, the tunnel felt claustrophobic—it was hard to imagine the dozens of people who had made their way through it in the past. Today, it looked as if the space hadn't been disturbed for decades.

"I remember my grandmother talking about her family's lagering cellars back in St. Louis," the sheriff said as they made their way slowly through the passage. "Before mechanical refrigeration, it wasn't uncommon for people to dig tunnels as a place to brew their alcohol. She told me that once refrigeration was available aboveground, though, many of the tunnels were abandoned or even demolished."

"Or forgotten, like these," Sadie said. "Do you think these are natural caves?"

"I don't think so," Roscoe said, ducking behind the others as he shined his light against the gray wall. "The space seems too rectangular and planned out."

Something scuffled in front of them.

"What is it?" Sadie paused, then shivered again as one of the flashlights caught a rat scurrying away. "You might have mentioned the fact that there could be vermin down here, but that doesn't mean I wanted to see one up close."

Edwin squeezed her shoulder.

"Makes it hard to believe this was once used for high-end clients looking for an evening of fun," Mac said.

Sadie continued down the narrow passage behind Roscoe, trying to imagine the men and women who'd once used this very tunnel. They'd likely gone from Main Street via the tunnels to the Browning House simply to avoid the stringent rules of Prohibition. And speakeasies weren't just a thing of the past. She'd read about modern-day speakeasies that paid tribute to America's Prohibition era. Just like in the twenties, they were difficult to find, with unmarked entrances and no signs. But for those who had the correct passcode, the dingy hallways led to cozy rooms where Frank Sinatra still played in the background.

"All a person needed to do was knock on the door of the shop and provide a password to gain entry," she said out loud, avoiding another large cobweb. "Customers would then be escorted through the tunnels to where they were treated to bootlegged alcohol. The secret tunnels allowed a quick getaway from the speakeasy, which would have had a warning-bell system."

"Watch your step," Mac said, pausing in front of them. "Here's another short flight of stairs."

Sadie took the sheriff's advice and went down the stairs slowly. She wondered how Edwin was faring, fitting his large frame into the small space. The last thing any of them needed was to stumble down the stone steps.

"Wait. I hear something, and it doesn't sound like a rat." Mac stopped, then held up his flashlight and shined it down the narrow passageway. "Is someone there?"

The beam of Sadie's flashlight picked up the form of a man pressed against the stone walls.

"Adam Solomon?" Mac called out as the man bolted and started running down the passageway away from them.

Sadie hurried up another short flight of stairs behind the sheriff and continued down the tunnel. She raised her flashlight until the white beam caught Adam's silhouette.

"Stop right there, Adam." The sheriff quickly moved farther down the tunnel. "I want you to stand still with your hands up in front of you."

Adam hesitated, then stepped out of the shadows, his hands in front of his face to block the light. A second later, he turned and started running down the tunnel again.

25

"HE'S GOING TO GET AWAY!" ROSCOE YELLED.

"I don't think so." Mac took another step forward.

Another flashlight shone back at them. Officer Kyle Kenmore stood blocking Adam's way a dozen yards ahead.

Adam looked back, clearly looking for a way of escape, but this time, despite the hidden door in the passageway, there was no way out. "I haven't done anything wrong. I just stumbled across these old tunnels."

"Oh, really?" the sheriff said. "I find that hard to believe."

Adam's jaw tightened. "I said I didn't do anything wrong."

"You mean, like convincing your niece you were here to help?" Sadie said. "And making her believe someone had broken into the Browning House, when all along it was you?"

"And don't forget breaking into my shop," Roscoe added. "And stealing the chess set."

"Did you find the missing fortune, Adam?" Sadie asked.

"You've got it all wrong."

"I think she's got it right, actually." Mac scowled. "And it's not going to be hard to prove, considering I have a video recording of you inside Putnam & Sons wearing the same hoodie you're wearing right now. But either way, I can still hold you. Turns out you're a wanted man."

Adam looked behind them down the darkened hall, but this time there was no way out. Clearly Adam Solomon wasn't the "favorite" uncle he claimed to be.

"Good work, Mac," Edwin said.

"How did you know to have Kyle waiting here?" Sadie asked, as the officer handcuffed the man.

"When you called to tell me what you'd discovered, it made sense that Adam could be hiding in the tunnel. And knowing there was a link between Putnam & Sons and the Browning House, I asked Kyle to see what he could find on that end."

"There's a hidden door in the back of one of the closets," Kyle said. "Took a little searching on my part, but I managed to find it. Of course, it helped that someone had left the door open a crack."

Roscoe chuckled. "Looks like the two of you were right on target."

The lights from the flashlights cast eerie shadows along the stone wall, but Sadie knew that the only ghost roaming these tunnels—and Putnam & Sons—was in the form of Adam Solomon.

"I never meant to hurt Ashley. Please believe that. All I wanted to do was access these tunnels, which the rest of the world has long forgotten. There's no crime in that."

"It's a crime to break into a place and steal things," Roscoe reminded him.

"I didn't think you'd notice."

"I might not have, if you wouldn't have left a trail of muddy footprints in my store," Roscoe said.

Adam's eyebrows rose in surprise.

"Why try to keep everything a secret?" Edwin asked. "Why didn't you just come forward from the beginning?"

Adam's shoulders slumped. "You wouldn't understand."

"Maybe we won't." Sadie shook her head. "But why don't you try to explain anyway?"

For the next sixty seconds, the only sound that came from the damp tunnel was the steady drip of water in the background. Sadie waited silently between Roscoe and the sheriff, hoping Adam would finally tell the truth behind what he'd been doing.

Adam gnawed on his lower lip for another few seconds, then shrugged, a marked look of defeat on his face. "My father used to tell me stories about his father, and his father's father, who were both involved with the Mountain Mafia, as well as bootlegging alcohol using these very tunnels. I knew one of the tunnels ran between the Browning House and one of the shops on Main Street. But that's all I knew. I didn't have a map, or a key...nothing."

"So you were using the house to try to access the other end of the tunnel?" Sadie asked.

"It took me a while to find the door. Whoever built the tunnel did a good job hiding it. Though, of course, knowing what they were trying to hide, it makes sense."

"What exactly were you looking for?" Sadie asked.

Adam slumped against the wall of the tunnel and stared at his feet. "Growing up, my grandfather was always telling me stories of living in Silver Peak during Prohibition. I always thought it was ironic that making the sale of alcohol illegal was supposed to *reduce* social problems. Instead of lowering crime and corruption, organized crime blossomed, prisons ended up being overcrowded, and add to that, there was an even greater number of corrupted police officers and public officials. Prohibition brought about very lucrative opportunities that my family was quick to take advantage of."

That was why Ashley's mother moved away, Sadie thought.

"One day," Adam continued, "things got out of hand. A police officer was killed right here on Main Street. I never knew for sure who actually committed the crime, but Louis Solomon—my great-grandfather—ended up being charged with the crime."

"Did he go to jail?" Roscoe asked.

"No, he disappeared. Rumor has it that he escaped and hid a large bag of cash somewhere in these tunnels, planning to come back for it at one point. As far as I know, he didn't make it back and no one has ever found it."

"But you thought *you* could find the money," Edwin said.

Adam's gaze dropped. "It should have been simple. Except my father decided to leave the house to Ashley, which complicated everything. I came up with a believable excuse to be here, but I had to search without her—or anyone for that matter—finding out what I was doing."

Sadie caught the anger in the man's voice. How sad that the idea of an inheritance could rip a family apart—for something that might or might not even exist.

"And my missing inventory?" Roscoe asked. "How did that play into the situation?"

"Once I discovered where the tunnel led and I found the door, I had free access to the hardware store." Adam met Roscoe's gaze. "I'm sorry. I just needed a few tools, and some flashlights, to help look for the money."

"What about the chess set?" Sadie asked, though the reason now seemed clear.

Adam hesitated again, but apparently he realized that whatever he didn't tell them now, they'd end up finding out eventually. "I finally had access to the tunnels, but I didn't have a map. I couldn't find the treasure, but I knew how much my father loved puzzles. I figured there might have been a connection between the house and the chess set since he left both of them to Ashley."

"Here's what I don't understand," Roscoe said. "People have been living in that house for decades. How come someone didn't stumble over the entrance after all this time?"

"It doesn't surprise me, actually," Adam said. "Unless you know what you're looking for, it's almost impossible to see. As I'm sure you've figured out, my great-grandfather was a master carpenter, and he used his skills to ensure it wasn't something people could simply stumble across."

"So then you decided to search for a second tunnel," Sadie said.

"Even before my father died, I was coming up here on weekends and searching. I figured if he was leaving the property to Ashley, there had to be something he wanted her to discover. But without the map, I was still lost."

Mac nodded at Kyle. "Go ahead. You're going to have some explaining to do. Breaking and entering, petty theft, and that doesn't even begin to address the fact that you're already a wanted man."

Sadie watched as the sheriff led Adam up another narrow row of steps into the Browning House, and she caught sight of Adam's muddy boots. Rainwater must have seeped into the tunnels, explaining one more missing piece of the puzzle.

The sun had almost set behind the mountains when Sadie stepped through the open closet door of the Browning House. She shivered, surprised at how cool the old, drafty house was.

"Uncle Adam?" Ashley stood at the bottom of the stairs, a startled expression on her face.

"Ashley." Her uncle turned around to face her.

"What's going on?" she asked.

"Your uncle found the tunnels," Mac said.

"Roz went on to bed, so I decided to come back to the house and finish up a few things." Ashley's fingers gripped the end of the railing, her face ashen. "They're arresting you? Why didn't you tell me about this? Why all the secrets?"

"I needed the money. I never meant to hurt you, Ashley. You have to believe that. But I'm in debt—to the wrong people. If there was a fortune inside these tunnels, I really needed to find it."

"Did Grandpa know about the tunnels?"

"I don't think so," Adam said. "But what I do know is that my father always hated that your mother took you away. He loved you—both of you."

"Why didn't he ever try to find me?" Ashley asked.

"I think he always hoped that you'd come back, but he wanted it to be your choice and not his. I think he also didn't want you to know about his involvement in..."

"All of his illegal activities?" The overhead light caught the tears in Ashley's eyes. "I have so many good memories of him. He gave me a love for puzzles and books, and I loved watching him work..."

"He would have liked to hear that."

"Instead I'm left with knowing he wasn't the man I thought he was."

"The two of you will have time to talk about all of this later. For now, Adam, you're coming with us," the sheriff finally said.

Ashley flipped on a couple of lights, then slipped out the front door onto the porch to watch the deputy and sheriff leave with her uncle.

"You think she's going to be okay?" Sadie asked Edwin as they took the stairs to the main floor. "It breaks my heart to think how betrayed she must feel."

"Why don't you go and talk with her?" Edwin suggested.

Sadie stepped outside onto the front porch of the Browning House and handed Ashley a package of tissues. Rain fell softly across the front lawn, bringing an extra coolness to the air and a reminder that winter wasn't far behind.

"Thanks."

"How are you doing?"

"I'm not sure. Right now, I'm kind of overwhelmed. And tired. So much of what I thought was true has turned out to be... well... lies."

"This has to be so hard."

Ashley's fingers gripped the porch railing. "I was so excited to find my mother's family. My grandfather had two sisters, Betty and Judith. Neither of them married, but when I showed up, they welcomed me like I had never been gone a day. Now all I can think about is, are they—and the rest of the family—involved in whatever Adam's involved in?"

Sadie struggled over how to respond. She couldn't fix this situation. "I'm so sorry, Ashley."

"Do you know how long I've longed to be a part of a big family? It was always just me and my mom growing up." Ashley shivered and shoved her hands into the pockets of her sweatshirt. "My mother never would tell me the real reason we left Colorado. Later I figured out that there must have been some kind of falling-out between her and her family, but I never guessed they were involved in bootlegging and the mafia. I guess I foolishly imagined finding my grandfather and living…I don't know…happily ever after. I wish my mother had told me the truth so I could have avoided all of this."

"Maybe she didn't want to tarnish the good memories you had of him," Sadie said.

"Maybe." Ashley looked up, the sadness in her expression caught in the white glow of the moonlight. "Before she died, I tried to talk to her again about why she wanted nothing to do with her father. She told me all she'd wanted to do was protect me, but by that point, I was an adult and wanted to be able to make my own decisions. For her sake, I waited until she passed away before I tried to find them. But by that time, it was too late.

"I guess the hardest part is feeling like such a fool," Ashley continued. "Like I was the only one who didn't know what was going on. Uncle Adam was simply trying to use me. And all of this for what? Some lost treasure that may or may not even exist. It just…it just makes me sad. Makes me feel as if I'm back to facing the world by myself."

"Human nature is interesting," Sadie said. "I've read some about the bootleggers and mafia members, and one of the things that struck me was that while they were involved on the wrong side of the law, many of them also cared deeply for their families and gave generously to charities and churches."

"That doesn't make sense."

"I'm not excusing their behavior. Maybe their actions were intended to make up for their sins, but they were still real people with loves and hurts and hopes." Sadie paused, struggling to put to words what she was thinking. "I guess what I'm trying to say is that whatever happened in the past...whoever your grandfather was or wasn't...clearly he cared about you. And from what I've heard, more than likely he was simply trying to honor your mother's wishes by staying out of your life."

"I hope you're right. Though I'm still trying to figure out why he gave me this house." Ashley took a step back, her brow furrowed. "Do you still have that key we found in the chess set?"

"Of course." Sadie dug in her pocket, then held up the key. "I just wish we knew what it opened."

"I'm probably crazy for saying this, but do you think there really is some hidden treasure buried somewhere in those tunnels like Adam believes?"

"I have no idea."

Ashley held up the key in front of her. "Because in spite of all that has happened, I can't stop wondering if there really is a buried treasure. Something my grandfather wanted me to find."

"It's possible," Sadie admitted, "but practically speaking, don't you think that anything that was—at one time—left in these tunnels is long gone?"

"You would think. But on the other hand, my grandfather must have believed there was truth to the story. He set all this up—the house, the photos, the chess set, the map—so I could find it."

"Kind of like a treasure hunt."

Ashley smiled for the first time all evening, but the light behind her eyes quickly dimmed. "It's a crazy idea, isn't it?"

"I don't know. There are hundreds of stories of lost treasure, some legend and some confirmed, and just as many rumored stories of treasures that are exactly that. Rumors. Yet people still look for them."

"Adam's been looking here for weeks, and he hasn't found anything," Ashley said. "Seems kind of naive to think I could find it myself."

"But Adam didn't have all the pieces to the puzzle," Sadie said. "That's why he needed the chess set."

"That's true. Which means we should have all the clues right here in front of us. Everything my grandfather left me in the will." Ashley gripped the key between her fingers. "What if we're wrong?"

"Then we don't find a treasure. But from my point of view, there's really nothing to lose at this point."

"We do have everything we need..."

Sadie smiled. "Then I say it's time we go on a treasure hunt."

26

Sadie set the map down on the kitchen table inside the Browning House while the oncoming storm rumbled in the background. Rain had already begun to pound against the windowpanes as the storm drove across the mountains and through Silver Peak.

"I say we wait to go back into the tunnels," Roscoe said as the lights flickered above them. "The storm is really strengthening."

Sadie shivered. "I'm not sure we have to wait, considering I'm not planning to leave any time soon with this downpour outside. And it won't make a difference down in the tunnels unless we discover they flood. We'd have to use the flashlights and lanterns no matter what was going on outside."

Sadie zipped up her warm fleece jacket. "Instead of going in blindly, though, I think we should at least study what we found. While the map is nothing more than a rough sketch, really, it does clearly show Silver Peak's Main Street, and the tunnels seem to be marked in blue."

"So going by that, here's the tunnel we used just now," Roscoe said, pointing to the map. "We know it runs from Putnam & Sons to this house, just like the map shows."

"How about some coffee while you all plot the course?" Ashley rubbed her hands together. "The temperatures are dropping, and it's going to get even colder in those tunnels."

"Sounds wonderful," Sadie and Roscoe said together.

Ashley turned on the electric kettle in the kitchen, then pulled out mugs from the cupboard while the rest of them studied the map on the dining room table.

"If we know where the first tunnel is now," Roscoe said, running his finger across the map. "Then the second one—assuming we're reading this correctly..."

"Is here." Sadie pointed to another line. "That has to be what Adam was looking for. The entrance to a second tunnel."

Ashley shook her head. "Without a map, you really would be lost down there."

"Here's something else," Edwin said, picking up the key off the table where Sadie had left it. "We didn't need a key for the first door. So this time, we might be looking for a keyhole."

"I didn't notice any keyholes while we were down there," Sadie.

"Even if there is one," Roscoe said, "it's going to be hard to find with all the dust and dirt down there."

"Or the key might go to something different entirely," Sadie threw out.

"Like?" Ashley asked.

"I don't know. Maybe some kind of box?"

"The box holding the missing bootlegged money," Ashley said, setting down a tray of chipped, mix-matched mugs in the middle of the table. "Sorry about these. They're not exactly fancy, but I do have cream and sugar."

"It's perfect," Sadie assured her, taking one of the mugs and adding a scoop of instant coffee.

Lightening struck in the distance, lighting up the night sky along with the dining room. Sadie scooted her chair forward an inch toward the table. No wonder why Ashley found the house creepy while she was here by herself. Especially knowing now that someone really had been coming and going at odd hours and searching the house.

"Can you tell where the second tunnel leads?" Ashley asked.

Sadie picked up the map and held it up to the light. "If I remember correctly, there used to be a house there, but it burned down back in the eighties, I believe. The owners torn it down, but it's still an empty lot."

"It's possible," Edwin said, adding another spoonful of sugar to his coffee, "that the tunnel collapsed when they tore it down."

Lightning flashed again, closer this time, followed by the rumble of thunder.

"I have something that might help." Ashley walked across the room and grabbed a bucket of paintbrushes. "You're right about there being plenty of dust and dirt after all these years. These should help uncover a keyhole—if there is one."

"Good idea," Sadie said. "I say we're good to go."

Sadie followed Roscoe back though the door, followed by Ashley. She shivered from the cold as she made her way down the uneven steps, trying to imagine men and women, dressed in their finest, coming and going through this tunnel from the store on Main Street to the speakeasy here at The Browning House.

"To be honest, I didn't particularly like this tunnel the first time and I'm not liking it any more now," Sadie said.

Edwin laughed. "I have to agree."

Roscoe stopped and held up his lantern. "Two thirds of the way down the tunnel, would roughly put the door... here."

"That sounds right," Sadie said.

"Logic says that the keyhole would be more or less waist high," Edwin said. "What if we at least make that a starting point?"

They divided out the wall in a grid of a few feet for each person and started the meticulous search of scouring the wall for anything that might show them where the second tunnel was. Sadie held a flashlight in one hand while using the thick brush in her other hand to wipe away bits of dust and spider webs that had formed along the wall over the decades. While she wasn't convinced they were going to discover the other tunnel—let alone a treasure—just the fact that they had stumbled on an unknown piece of Silver Peak's history fascinated her.

And ferrying people through the tunnels clearly wasn't the only thing that had happened here. Bootleggers had secretly transported liquor and other goods prohibited during the 1920s and early 1930s through these underground passageways. There were also probably gentlemen, wanting to visit other unscrupulous businesses, like a house of ill repute, where the *proper* gentleman would walk into a legitimate business and end up at a brothel with no one being any the wiser.

She frowned at the thought. Clearly, people hadn't changed all that much.

"I wonder how long it's been since anyone has been here—besides Adam, anyway," Ashley asked, working beside Sadie.

Sadie sneezed. "According to the amount of dust still on these walls, I'd say decades."

"I'm still trying to wrap my mind around the fact that they've been here for all of these decades, and I had no clue," Roscoe said.

"These won't be a secret after today." Sadie leaned over to brush away another section. "Just wait until the *Chatterbox* gets wind of this story. People are going to have a heyday with this."

"And what about Troy?" Roscoe said. "He'll have this on the front page of the next issue of the *Silver Peak Sentinel*."

"We'll have visitors coming for miles and miles to check these tunnels out," Edwin added.

Sadie laughed. "Silver Peak could always use the tourism boost."

Towns like Silver Peak relied heavily on tourist coming through for the stunning mountain scenery, but also the hot springs pools, tours of the old mines, some which were even still operation. A pair of tunnels left over from the early twentieth century would be a huge draw.

Sadie continued making her way to the end of her section without finding anything. Either they were looking in the wrong place or there wasn't another tunnel.

"Maybe we're wrong about the door and the second tunnel," Sadie suggested, taking a step back before she moved onto another spot.

"It does seem that Adam would have found something by now..."

"Wait..." Light from the lanterns cast eerie shadows against the wall. "I think I might have found something."

"Where?" Roscoe asked.

"Right here." Sadie's heart pounded. "This stone is loose. It might not be anything, but if we could wedge it loose..."

"I've got a pocketknife." Roscoe handed Sadie the knife, then held up his lantern while Sadie worked to unwedge the loose piece. After a minute of working at it, a small section of the wall popped out into Sadie's hand revealing a keyhole.

"Where's the key?" Sadie asked.

Sadie dug into her pocket and pulled it out, then looked to Ashley. "Maybe you should do the honors."

Ashley hesitated. "It could be nothing but another empty tunnel."

"Maybe. Or there could be a treasure your grandfather wanted you to find."

Sadie held up her lantern while Ashley slid the key into the hole. Something clicked. "It definitely fits."

A moment later, they pushed open the door that only a few moments before had been completely hidden.

"At least we know the map was right," Sadie said, stepping inside and wondering if they were going to find anything more than just a tunnel this time.

A stream of lights down the narrow passageway showed another dingy, dusty tunnel.

"We can go inside," Roscoe said, "but it looks to me like just another dead end."

Twenty yards ahead, the light hit a wall. It was a dead end.

Roscoe ran his hand over the stones. "It looks as if it's become blocked over the years."

Something white flashed in Sadie's peripheral vision.

"Wait a minute..." Sadie lowered her flashlight, searching for whatever it was she'd just seen. "I think there's something here."

Roscoe, Edwin, and Ashley were right beside her, pulling off a pile of loose rocks.

"It's some old wooden boxes with white labels." Sadie brushed off the top of one of them. "This looks like the box the man was carrying in the photo I found in your books, Ashley."

"Why don't we carry them to the house," Roscoe suggested. "We'll be able to see what we've got better."

Sadie dusted off the top of one of the boxes that was the size of a file box, sneezed, then balanced her flashlight on top so she could see where she was going.

Back at the house, rain was still pattering against the window as Sadie set the first of the three wooden boxes on the dining room table, then took a step back.

Ashley stood beside Sadie, her eyes wide with excitement. "Do you really think they're filled with some kind of treasure?"

"We won't know until we open them up."

Roscoe pulled out his pocketknife and pried open the first box.

"Well?" Ashley said.

"Looks like left over supplies from Prohibition," Sadie said, pulling out a piece of paper from the top. "This is a medicinal whiskey prescription form, the only way to legally drink during Prohibition."

"That's not very useful today, now is it?" Roscoe laughed.

"And look at this," Sadie laughed as she pulled out an unopened bottle of *Mock Whiskey.* "This one's even got its federal tax-stamp intact."

"Is any of this worth money?" Ashley asked.

Sadie hesitated, knowing she was going to disappoint the young woman. "There might be collectors who would be interested in some of this, but as far as monetary value, not really. This definitely isn't the cache of missing cash you were hoping for."

Ashley sat down on one of the dining room chairs, clearly disappointed. "Or maybe the rumors about the treasure were never true."

"Or someone beat us to it," Edwin said.

"I'm not so sure you didn't find a treasure after all," Sadie said, sitting down in one of the chairs.

Ashley's gaze narrowed. "What do you mean?"

"When you went to Edwin and asked him about the city restoring your historic property, he didn't see the value of this property beyond what it is... a rundown house. But now, I have a feeling the discovery of these tunnels might change everything."

"What do you mean?" Ashley asked.

"While I have no idea if this is what your grandfather wanted for you, but what if he just wanted you to discover the tunnels. You might be able to sell this property as a valued historical landmark considering what it's connected to."

"Do you think so?" Ashley plopped into one of the empty chairs beside her.

"I think Sadie's right," Edwin said. "This is a place where tourists could come and go through the tunnels, showcasing how it was used by outlaws and the stolen money that was never found, a house of ill repute during the peak of the silver mining, and a speakeasy in the twenties."

"Which means I might actually come out of all of this with a profit." Ashley smiled then turned to Roscoe. "Which reminds me of one other thing. As a small token of my appreciation I want to give you something."

"Me?" Roscoe glanced at Sadie. "I don't understand. You didn't have to get me anything, Ashley."

"Yes, I do. I feel bad about the whole chess set incident, so I wanted to give you one of my grandfather's wooden puzzles. I know it's not the chess set, but I thought you might appreciate it."

"Are you sure?" Roscoe asked, taking the gift.

"Yes. I'm very sure. I'll warn you, though. It isn't easy. You have to take it apart, then reassemble it."

"Sounds like a fun challenge," Roscoe said. "Thank you."

Ashley's smile broadened. "You're welcome."

Sadie rested her arm around the girl's shoulders. "How are you doing, now that all of this is over? It's been an emotional few weeks."

"Yes, it has, but I think I'm going to be okay. I feel for Adam. I saw him as family, but I'm not going to let this get in the way of getting to know the rest of the Solomon family."

"I think that's a good decision," Sadie said.

"And in the meantime," Ashley wrapped her arm around Sadie's waist. "I feel as if I've gained a family right here in Silver Peak."

27

Early Monday evening, Sadie set out a bowl of potato salad—fresh from the Market—on the long table that was already filled with plates, silverware, and more mouth-watering food on the back patio of her house. Roz—who was feeling much better—and Sara were watching Roscoe and Theo play a competitive game of chess in the back corner while she and Alice set out dinner and Edwin grilled the burgers.

She always loved the informal gatherings with friends and family, and had decked out her patio with a standard, coal grill, and Adirondack chairs. And today the weather had decided to cooperate. It was just warm enough to be able to enjoy an early afternoon get-together while overlooking the mountain forest view.

Something in the distance caught her eye. Sadie turned from the table to watch a golden eagle glide by, wings lifted and wingtip feathers spread out like fingers. The stunning view of the mountain forest never failed to take her breath away. Never failed to remind her of how deeply blessed she was.

"The burgers are almost done." Edwin came up beside Sadie and nudged her gently with his shoulder. "Today turned out perfectly, didn't it?"

She smiled up at him. "Meaning the weather or the company?"

Edwin smiled. "Both, but most definitely the company."

"I would have to agree. And the perfect ending to what was, shall we say, a challenging couple of weeks."

A section of the grill caught fire from the grease, and Edwin quickly moved two of the burgers from the back to the front. "I haven't had the chance to ask you how things ended with Marge and the notorious bedroom set."

Sadie laughed. After almost two weeks of hard work—including the emotional drama that always came with Marge—she was pleased to be able to report a happy ending. "I delivered the bedroom set to her this morning."

"And Marge... was she happy?"

Sadie caught the hesitation in Edwin's voice and smiled. "She was speechless. In a good way."

"Marge. Speechless. I find that hard to believe."

Sadie laughed. "Then she thanked me. Up until the very end I think she was convinced it wasn't going to be what she wanted. But the best part is that I believe we've come to an understanding. Marge will always be Marge—prickly and all—but at least I understand her a little better."

While Sadie had no plans to jump into another one of Marge's projects any time soon, at least she'd be more understanding when she was around the other woman. But things had turned out okay all around. She'd even run into Bill who told her his wife wanted him to come home.

"I'm glad to hear you worked things out with Marge." Edwin reached out and squeezed her hand, sending warm shivers through her. "Understanding where the other person's coming from is often half the battle."

Sadie smiled. "She even promised me a tour of the new bedroom once her family leaves, but for now it sounds like she has her hands full."

"Does she get along with them?"

"I believe there have been a few unmet expectations over the years, but knowing Marge, she'll manage."

"I think you're right." Edwin leaned against the balcony rail while the savory scent of simmering hamburgers filled the air.

Sadie glanced at the table, mentally checking off everything she and Alice had planned to serve. Potato salad, fruit salad with a generous helping of raspberries, baked beans, condiments, red-velvet bar cookies from The Market, and a jug of lemonade.

"How long for the burgers?" Sadie asked. "I think everything else is ready."

"I was just told we needed to wait until Roscoe and Theo finish their chess game. According to Roscoe, they're just about done." He went ahead and moved the burgers to the cooler sides of the grill before closing the lid to keep them warm.

Across the patio, Roscoe and Theo hovered over the board anticipating their next moves, while everyone else looked on.

"It's turning out to be a pretty intense game," Edwin said.

Sadie laughed. "With Roscoe and Theo involved, I'm not surprised."

"By the way, I think I might have to challenge you to a game later this evening. I was impressed with your win against Roscoe, though I have to warn you that I have a few tricks of my own."

"Do you now?" Sadie laughed. "Challenge accepted, though don't be too overly confident, Mr. Mayor. You're on."

"I look forward to it."

Sadie leaned against the rail next to Edwin, content to soak up the afternoon sun in the company of those she loved.

"I saw the sheriff this morning," Edwin said. "Adam's been transferred to Denver where he's facing charges of racketeering, and tax evasion for starters."

"I have to say I'm still surprised at how all of this turned out. Adam seemed like the perfect gentleman. Crazy to think that instead he was the perfect scammer."

"According to the sheriff, he's been involved in Ponzi schemes, investment fraud, and everything else you can imagine in between. I guess he thought he'd be safe in a little town like Silver Peak."

"Turned out he was wrong." Sadie shook her head. She almost felt sorry for the guy except for knowing how many people he'd hurt. Especially Ashley. "What saddens me is how Ashley ended up being just another victim on his list. Just when she thought she'd found her family."

Sadie turned and looked up as the back door to the house slammed shut.

"Speaking of Ashley," Edwin said.

"I thought I heard a party going on back here." Ashley walked onto the back patio, wearing jeans and a warm red sweater and a smile on her face.

Sadie crossed the patio to great her guest. "I'm so glad you were able to make it."

"Thank you so much for inviting me. It smells wonderful."

"You're just in time. Dinner is just about ready." Sadie gave the girl a hug. Roz, Alice, and the others greeted Ashley, then went back to the chess game.

"You wouldn't think people could generate so much noise over a chess game," Sadie said with a laugh before turning back to Ashley. "I really am glad you were able to come. I wasn't sure how long you were going to be in town."

"I'm leaving tomorrow morning, actually, but I will be back."

"Wonderful. I know the past few weeks have been very tough for you."

"They have been, but I've also learned that the Solomon family is big, and not all of them were involved in the shady business deals like my uncle was."

Roscoe walked over and stood in front of Ashley. "The last few days have reminded me how much I enjoy chess."

"Game over?" Sadie asked.

"Yes, but it was a close one," Roz said.

"My grandfather would have loved playing a round with you." Ashley's smile broadened. "So who won?"

"I managed to put the boy in his place," Roscoe said, grabbing Theo around the shoulders in a playful hug, "but let me tell you, it wasn't easy. You've got some good strategies there, Theo. We'll have to play again sometime."

Theo beamed. "Definitely."

"Would you all mind if I said something before dinner?" Ashley cleared her throat. "I'm not much for speeches, but I have some good news—several pieces of good news, actually—I'd like to share with all of you."

"Of course," Sadie said.

Everyone turned their attention to Ashley.

"I just wanted to thank you...each one of you for what you've done to help me over the past couple of weeks." Ashley's voice broke with emotion. "I came to Silver Peak struggling, with little direction in my life. My plan was to find my grandfather. Instead, I discovered he'd died. I was so crushed I didn't have the opportunity to see him again before he passed away. Then I had to deal with the problems with the house... It seemed as if there were so many uncertainties that I didn't know how to deal with. To be honest I panicked.

"But then all of you, for whatever reasons, befriended me. I've never lived in a small town like Silver Peak, but I've already fallen in love with the people here. Where else can you eat out at family-run restaurants on one corner and visit a Victorian opera house on another. Then there's the park, the local library, and the *Chatterbox*... In fact, even after I leave I'll still be reading the blog just to keep up on what everyone's up to."

Everyone laughed, then waited for her to continue.

"I guess what I really want to say is thank you. All of you. From the bottom of my heart.

Sadie stepped forward and gave her a hug. "We're just glad to have gotten to know you."

"What's your good news?" Roz asked.

"Well, first of all, the house sold."

"Already?" Roz said.

"Yes. An investor in Denver was looking for something historic to fix up and with the discovery of the tunnels, he believes the tourists who come through Silver Peak will absolutely love the story."

"I agree," Sadie said. "That's fantastic."

"Everything has come together so quickly that my head is spinning, but I've decided to go ahead with a longtime dream to set up an online store. Thanks to Sadie, in particular, who introduced me to some people around town. Josh has helped me secure the services of several woodworkers, specifically several people he recommended who have been out of work and needed a second chance...like I did. Bill, for example, is one of Sadie's tenants who used to work in construction and has skills as a cabinetmaker. When I talked to him about what I wanted to do he was so excited. So I can still hardly believe it, but I think this is really going to work out."

"What kinds of things will you be selling?" Roz asked.

"All kinds of wooden puzzles and toys for children. I'll be in charge of the product ideas, many of them coming from things that my grandfather showed me. Oh, and Marie Campbell..."

"Ricky's mom?" Roscoe asked.

"Yes," Ashley said. "She's going to work with me as well. She needed a job where she could work at home, and it turns out she's a genius with computers. She'll be running the online store and getting it set up. After that, I might look at starting up a physical store, maybe even here in Silver Peak."

"All I can say, Ashley, is that I'm so thrilled things are coming together for you," Sadie said, unable to stop smiling.

"Do you know where you'll be staying?" Alice asked.

"For now, I'll be splitting my time among my new family here. Marie's father has an extra room they'll rent to me, so it helps all of us."

"It sounds as if everything's working out," Edwin said.

Ashley took in a deep breath. "I honestly had come to the point where I didn't believe any of this was possible, and while I wish my grandfather was still alive—and things had turned out different with Adam—God has shown me that he still cares. And he's used people like you to do that."

"I have a feeling he would have been very happy with the woman you've become," Roz said.

"Oh, Ashley," Sadie said, "I have something for you as well. I almost forgot. A package came to my address, but it was addressed to you. I set it on the chair over here."

A moment later Sadie returned with the package that had come this afternoon.

"It's from my grandfather's sister. She told me she was sending me something, but didn't want to tell me what it was over the phone. I hope you didn't mine my giving her your address."

"Not at all."

Ashley pulled off the brown paper to reveal a shoebox. Inside was a stack of letters neatly tied with a piece of twine. She held up one of the letters, then ran her finger across the return address.

"Danny Solomon." She looked up at Sadie. "These are letters from my grandfather."

"Adam mentioned he'd written you letters."

"Yes, but..." Ashley started flipping through the envelopes one by one. "They all say return to sender. They must be letters my mother returned."

"Your grandfather must have saved them all these years," Roz said.

"Wait..." Ashley picked up a slip of paper. "There's a separate letter here. It's from my grandfather's sister."

Sadie rested her hand on Ashley's shoulder. "Would you like some privacy?"

"No, it's okay." Ashley looked up at Sadie and smiled, but Sadie didn't miss the glint of tears in the girl's eyes as she started reading the letter out loud.

My dearest Ashley,

I found this stack of letters in some of your grandfather's things shortly after he died. Your grandfather wasn't perfect, but he was a good, kind man who had a big heart. He loved his family, and he loved you and your mother. I only wish that things hadn't ended the way they did. I had always hoped that the two of you could have somehow connected before he died, but he never wanted to push your mother. All I can hope is that these letters will somehow bridge the gap that others created between the two of you. He spoke of you so often and I think in many ways you were the inspiration to him in taking the family business legitimate. You made him a better man in the end.

Please know that you are always welcome to come to visit and will always be a part of the Solomon family.

Sincerely,
Betty Solomon

"Wow...I...I don't know what to say, except that he didn't forget about me." She held up the stack of letters and smiled.

"Oh, Ashley. I hope this gives you the closure you've needed."

"I think I feel the sorriest for my mother. I know she loved him, but she was also stubborn. I guess she took after my grandfather." Ashley smiled through her tears. "I just wish they could have solved their differences before they both died. But these letters… I'll save them for later. I don't think you all will want to watch me blubber through them."

Sadie squeezed her shoulder gently, understanding. "You're going to stay for dinner, aren't you?"

"I really just planned to come by and say good-bye. I have so much to do before I leave… "

"You've still got to eat," Roz said. "Stay long enough to at least grab a bite."

Ashley hesitated, then nodded. "All right."

"And in the meantime," Sadie said. "If there's anything you need. Anything at all… "

Ashley reached up and gave Sadie a hug. "Thank you. Thank you for everything."

"Anyone ready for some burgers?" Edwin asked, lifting the cover on the grill.

Sadie smiled as Edwin began serving up the hamburgers, then sent up a prayer of thanks for friends, and family, and the wonderful sense of community He'd blessed them with.

About the Author

Carol Jefferson is the pen name for a team of writers who have come together to create the series Mysteries of Silver Peak. Lisa Harris is a Christy Award winner for *Dangerous Passage*, a Christy Award finalist for *Blood Ransom*, and the winner of the Best Inspirational Suspense Novel for 2011 from *Romantic Times*. She has sold over thirty novels and novella collections. She and her family have spent over ten years living as missionaries in Africa where she works with the women and runs a nonprofit organization that works alongside their church-planting ministry. When she's not working she loves hanging out with her family, cooking different ethnic dishes, photography, and heading into the African bush on safari. For more information about her books and life in Africa, visit her Web site at lisaharriswrites.com or her blog at myblogintheheartofafrica.blogspot.com.

Read on for a sneak peek of another exciting book in Mysteries of Silver Peak!

Lights and Shadows

SADIE FIDDLED WITH THE CONDIMENTS AND WATCHED THE OTHER customers flooding into Flap Jack's. She read the front and back of the stand-up card advertising dessert pancakes. She took a sip of her coffee and listened with amusement as Marge Ruxton, at the next table, described her recent shopping trip to Denver to the friend with whom she was having breakfast. Mostly she watched the door.

"Sure you don't want to order?" Diana, the red-haired waitress, reached out with the coffeepot and topped off Sadie's mug.

"Roz is supposed to join me, but she seems to be running late." Sadie glanced at her watch. "I'll give her a call and see if she's on her way."

"Sure. Just give me the high sign if you want to order." Diana smiled and moved on to the next table.

Sadie took out her phone and called her best friend's cell.

"Hi, Sadie."

Roz's greeting sounded as though she had played it in slow motion.

"Roz? Are you coming? I'm at Flap Jack's."

Roz sighed. "I don't know."

"What's the matter?" Sadie sat up straighter, alert to Roz's listlessness and wishing she could see her. "Are you behind this morning?"

"Something like that. I'm not dressed yet."

"What?" That wasn't like Roz. Still, Sadie didn't want to tie up one of Diana's tables much longer during the rush hour. "You sound like you don't want to go out for breakfast. Why don't I come over to your house?"

"Sure," Roz said. "Thanks, Sadie."

Sadie signed off and took another mouthful of coffee. She put a few dollars on the table, stood, and waved to Diana. The waitress was in the middle of taking an order, but Sadie made sure she saw her before she strode out the door. Her Tahoe was parked out front, and she climbed in. It took her only a couple of minutes to reach the Putnam house.

Roz opened the door still in her fuzzy bathrobe and slippers.

"Hi. I'm sorry."

"Don't be." Sadie gave her a hug and then moved into the entry. "Come on. I'll make us something to eat."

"You don't have to."

"Of course not," Sadie said with a chuckle, "but I'm starved."

Roz laughed and led her to the kitchen.

"What would you have ordered if we were at Flap Jack's?" Sadie asked.

"*Mmm*. Probably pancakes with raspberry sauce."

"Got any raspberries?"

"No," Roz said, "but there's a quart of strawberries in the fridge."

Sadie grabbed an apron off the towel rack and tied it around her waist.

"If you're going to be this way, I guess I'd better help." Roz opened a cupboard and took down a box of pancake mix.

Sadie knew her way around Roz's kitchen nearly as well as she did her own, and she soon had a skillet heating and batter ready to pour. Meanwhile, Roz had sat down at the table and was slicing fresh strawberries into a bowl. When Sadie had half a dozen near-perfect pancakes ready, she carried the serving plate over and untied the apron.

"Just let me get the coffee."

She poured for both of them, while Roz divvied the pancakes.

"You must be feeling better," Sadie observed as Roz smothered her own hotcakes with sweetened strawberries.

"Who can stay depressed with you around?"

Sadie sat down. Her mission was not complete, but she was making good progress. After asking a brief blessing, she took a bite.

"These are really good," Roz agreed after her first taste. "Thanks a lot, Sadie."

Sadie gazed at her across the table. "You're welcome. Now tell me. What had you so down this morning?"

Roz grimaced. "Have you read the *Chatterbox* lately?"

Sadie shook her head and cut another bite with her fork. "What does it say?"

Roz reached for her smartphone and tapped a few buttons on the screen. "Here's the latest." She handed it over to Sadie.

The Chatterbox was an online gossip blog. No one in Silver Peak knew who authored the stream of tidbits, or at least no one admitted knowing. But the *Chatterbox* seemed to get wind of every celebration, scandal, or feud in town.

Sadie frowned at the screen as she read: *A movie company is coming to Silver Peak! That old cult classic we all either love or hate,* Stranger from a Strange World, *is going to be remade in the same setting where it was done fifty years ago. Break out your bellbottoms and your* My Favorite Martian *lunchbox. It's coming, friends! Or are they among us already?*

She couldn't help a wry smile that tugged at her lips. "Cute. But I can see why that would give you pause. Edwin told me a while back that the studio was thinking of doing a remake."

Roz said nothing but lifted her mug, took a sip of coffee, and set it down carefully on the table.

Sadie hadn't wanted to admit it, but the mention of the old film had filled her mind with recollections too. Obviously, it had hit Roz with more force, and she shouldn't be surprised. She laid down the phone. "I'm sorry, Roz. It must be hard for you, with all the memories this brings up."

"You could say that." She looked up at Sadie, her eyes filled with pain.

"I didn't mean to make light of it."

"I know. The worst part for me is, hardly anyone even remembers Mike."

"That's not true," Sadie said. "Honey, lots of people in town remember your brother."

"Nobody ever mentions him. And if the topic does come up, everyone clams up or changes the subject."

Sadie reached over and grasped her hand. "Mike Tabor was one of the nicest boys I ever knew. People may be uncomfortable with thinking about how he died, but that does not mean they've forgotten him."

Roz blinked back tears. "Do you think about him much?"

"Sometimes. But I admit, it's not as often as I used to." Sadie sat back with a sigh. She had realized recently that days went by when she didn't even think much about T.R., her dear husband who had been gone several years, let alone Mike Tabor. "Time does that. I think it's a blessing, really, or we'd be constantly in despair. God eases our sorrow and lets us look beyond it to the future."

"I suppose you're right." Roz picked up her fork and toyed with a piece of pancake on her plate. "But to me, it seems impossible that anyone could forget something like that."

"They haven't. But after all, we were twelve. We were very impressionable. Remember how excited we were when we first heard that a movie was going to be filmed in Silver Peak?"

Roz smiled grudgingly. "I thought it would be the most wonderful summer ever."

Sadie nodded. "We used to go and watch the movie people every chance we got, and get as close to the set as they would let us."

"I'm afraid I didn't get much else done that summer. And when Mike came home to supper one night and told us he'd gotten on as an extra—well, that was the icing on the cake."

"Yeah, that was so much fun." Sadie smiled, thinking about how jealous she and her friends had been when they had learned that a few local people had chances to be in the film.

"I know it may sound flaky," Roz said, "but I've wondered all these years if Mike's death was really an accident."

Sadie shifted uneasily in her chair. She had heard this suggestion from Roz before, but it had been years since they had spoken of it.

"Do you really think that?"

Roz shrugged. "I don't know."

"Your dad was a police officer," Sadie said gently. "They investigated it thoroughly."

"Did they?" Roz's chin came up a stubborn fraction of an inch. "He never would tell me what they found."

"Honey, you were so young. He probably didn't want to trouble you any worse with the details. He and your mom probably figured it was bad enough that you lost your only brother. And besides, things were different back then. Grownups didn't discuss things like that with kids."

"It's not like we were babies."

"I know. But twelve is pretty young." Sadie sighed. "Your father did see the police reports, I'm sure. He must have been satisfied."

"He never told me anything." Roz gulped. "I asked him about it lots of times, but he would just brush it aside and say something like, 'You don't need to get all worked up about it, Rosalind.' I hated that. I wanted to know every detail."

"Of course you did." Sadie's heart ached as she gazed at her friend's anguished features.

"I'm not saying Mike was murdered. But I'm not saying he wasn't, either. Maybe it was criminal negligence—but if so, why wasn't anyone charged? If it was something besides a freak accident, why can't I know that? I just want to be sure of what really happened. Is that too much to ask?"

"No, it's not. But we'll probably never know for certain what happened." Sadie considered things for a moment. "Of course, this is very important to you. Why don't I see if I can find out anything you didn't already know?"

Roz's shoulders drooped. "You don't have to. It would probably lead nowhere anyway."

"I don't mind asking a few questions."

"I know I'm being crazy right now," Roz said. "You're a busy lady, and I wouldn't ask you to spend your time on this. Although, you are pretty good at finding out things. But this is something that happened fifty years ago."

Sadie lifted her coffee cup and took a sip. This had bothered Roz for so long, she knew deep down that her friend would not be at peace unless she learned more about her brother and why he died when he did. She smiled at Roz.

"That's what I'm best at—historical events."

"If you're sure, it would mean a lot to me." Roz leaned across the table. "You know some odd things happened right around the time Mike died. It was only two days after he replaced that actor who'd been fired, Sadie. Two days. I've never been able to shake off the feeling that the guy who was fired might have had something to do with it."

"Really? I never thought of that."

"Why not?"

Sadie shook her head helplessly. "I guess because I assumed the police thoroughly questioned him."

"Maybe. But how do we know? Maybe there was someone else in the cast who had hoped to get that part, but Mike got it instead.

And there was another kid at school who had it in for Mike. Do you remember the cheating scandal?"

"Vaguely."

"Well, there you go. That's a lot of bad feelings against my brother. It's called motive."

"Now, Roz..."

"I'm not saying anyone meant to kill Mike. But what if someone wanted to give him a little shove so he'd mess up the scene, just to make him look bad? Something like that, maybe. Or a prank gone wrong."

Sadie let out a deep breath. "I'll make a few inquiries, but there might not be anything there to learn."

Roz's mouth twitched, but she nodded. "I understand."

"Okay. Now, finish your breakfast and go hit the shower. I'll clean up the kitchen while you get dressed."

"You don't need to do all that."

"Well, I'm doing it. And I will think about everything you've said and see if I can find out anything. Maybe Mac can help me, although he wasn't around when it happened."

Roz brightened. "That's a great idea. The sheriff would come at it without prejudice, since he wasn't part of the investigation."

Sadie held up one hand. "Remember, I'm not promising anything."

"Okay." Roz picked up her fork. "And thank you. I really appreciate it."

Twenty minutes later, Roz came back to the kitchen dressed in designer jeans and a plaid blouse.

"Feel better?" Sadie asked, giving her a little hug. "You look great."

"Thanks. I do feel better now."

"Want to come over to the store for a while?"

Roz shook her head. "Not just now. Maybe later."

"Okay. I'd better get going, but call me if you want to talk again." Sadie picked up her purse and headed out the door.

Once she arrived at the Antique Mine on Main Street, she went into high gear. She had a lot to do today—new stock to log and display, online ads to prepare, and upcoming sale flyers and auction catalogs to browse, so she could plan her next buying sprees. That was in addition to the usual summer flow of tourists at the shop.

Her assistant Julie breezed in a few minutes after Sadie arrived. "Morning!"

"Hi, Julie. Could you help me get these new things out before we open? I'm running a little late this morning."

"Oh, and tonight's the big night, isn't? The dinner theater, I mean?"

"Yes. Are you and Chad going?"

"Planning on it," Julie said. "I hear the play's really funny."

Sadie was looking forward to the evening out with Edwin Marshall. The refurbished opera house was the perfect venue for dinner theater productions. Sadie was on the Preservation Committee that had overseen the restoration, and she sometimes helped write scripts for the local players, but tonight she would be watching someone else's work for fun.

"Great. We'll see you there."

"These are cool." Julie's eyes danced as she removed a set of carved jade bookends from a box.

"They're not that old, but I thought they'd catch someone's eye." The sight of the stone lions made Sadie smile. For some reason, she'd found it hard to pass up the garage sale owner's souvenir of Hong Kong, even though she knew the bookends were crafted for the tourist trade. "And the price was right," she added.

"Speaking of cool, did you hear about the movie?" Julie asked. "They're going to film right here in Silver Peak."

"Yeah, I did." Julie was too young to remember the original frenzy of filming the science fiction classic. Sadie wasn't surprised that Julie was excited about it. "It should bring in some extra business. Maybe we'll get some aliens in here to buy souvenirs before they head home to Mars."

Julie laughed. "Maybe we should stock postcards that say, 'Greetings from Earth.'"

"That's a good one." Sadie reached into another box. "Now, where do you think these pewter plates should go? With the china or with the Americana?"

That evening, Sadie dressed with care. An evening at the opera house always felt special, and she put on one of her best dresses, blue with shimmery silver threads in the bodice. She wasn't much for wearing makeup, but she applied a little lipstick and blow-dried her short hair just enough to give it some body.

Edwin's car crunched gravel in the driveway, and Hank heard it too. He barked once, and Sadie heard him leave his bed in the kitchen and pad to the front door. The faithful golden retriever was waiting in the entry when she went downstairs. The bell rang just before she reached the door.

Edwin's eyes lit when she swung the door open. "Hi. You look terrific."

"Thanks," Sadie said with a smile. "Let me grab my purse."

The night's entertainment was the first dinner theater production of the summer, and Sadie knew that tickets for the play had sold out. The room quickly filled with local residents, all of whom seemed upbeat and eager for a fun evening. Sadie enjoyed talking to friends and seeing people she usually saw in jeans and flannel shirts turned out in regal style. She and Edwin took small portions of goodies from the appetizer bar and mingled with the others.

The first act of the play was announced, and they found their seats. Julie and Chad joined them at their table for eight, along with Martin and Paula Deering and Jane and Jerry Remington. Martin was the song leader at Campfire Chapel, and Paula was the church pianist. Jerry and Jane owned the Silver Peak Bed & Breakfast. The Remingtons had also been instrumental in the restoration of the opera house.

"Everything looks wonderful in here," Sadie said to Jane.

"Doesn't it?" Jane grinned. "The committee put in hundreds of hours getting everything just right for this season."

"Well, the Preservation Committee certainly brought the opera house back to its old glory," Edwin said.

The lights dimmed for a moment, and everyone stopped talking. Luz Vidal, who was chairman of the opera house board's program committee for the season, stood at the end of the hall near the stage. "Welcome to the new season at the Silver Peak Opera House. We hope you're pleased with tonight's show."

Sadie enjoyed the first act of the play and found herself laughing along with the others as the zany plot unfolded. Tonight's production was a light comedy, and she was almost glad it wasn't something that would require her to think, though she loved the interactive mysteries that were sometimes presented.

At the intermission, their main course of chicken Kiev was served. The diners talked about the play for a few minutes, and then began to catch up on each other's family news.

Edwin leaned closer to Sadie. "I don't think I told you that Noelle and Carl have bought their plane tickets. They'll arrive on Friday."

"How nice," Sadie said. Edwin had not seen his daughter for several months, and she knew he looked forward to showing Noelle what he had done with the old family home. "I'll be happy to see them again. Will they be here long enough for us to spend some time together?"

"She said they're planning on a couple of weeks."

"Great." Already Sadie was mentally planning a family dinner at her house and a fun afternoon showing Noelle around the Antique Mine.

"How are you doing, Edwin?" Paula asked from across the table. "Are your mayoral duties keeping you busy?"

"Not too bad," Edwin replied. "I was just telling Sadie that my daughter and her family are coming to visit soon."

"That's great," Paula said.

"Will they be staying with you?" Jane asked.

"Oh yes," Edwin said, smiling broadly. "I wouldn't let them go anywhere else."

"That's a good thing," Jerry told him. "The B and B is filled to capacity next week. I guess you've heard about the movie crew that's coming."

"So soon?" Sadie asked.

Jerry nodded. "Yes, they've got everything planned, and the director's ready to start."

Edwin said, "I attended a meeting with the opera house board recently to talk about what we can do to welcome them. They're quite excited about it, and they're going to see if the film studio will actually hold the premiere here next spring, when the film releases."

"Wouldn't that be something?" Paula said.

The others agreed with her. Sadie didn't chime in, but kept her thoughts to herself. The more hoopla surrounding the movie, the more memories would be stirred up. She hoped she could find out something that would ease Roz's misgivings. She let the others chatter on about the film, the actors, and the flurry of business the enterprise would bring to Silver Peak.

A comment from Jerry caught her attention. "Hey, wouldn't it be great if they showed the old movie—the one they're doing the remake from?"

"Ooh, I like that idea," Jane said. "We could have a showing here at the opera house. Everyone in town could see the classic now."

Paula nodded. "I've never seen it, but now I want to."

"It would be fresh in everyone's minds when the new one comes out," Jerry said.

Sadie kept her eyes on her plate to avoid giving away her dismay. She knew at least one person who would not love this idea—Roz Putnam. At least she could forewarn her friend, so she would have time to get used to the idea.

The dishes were cleared, and the lights flickered, signaling that the second act of the play was about to begin. Sadie wasn't sorry. She turned her chair slightly so that she had a better view of the stage.

When the play had finished, they all applauded enthusiastically.

"Not too cerebral, but good, fun entertainment," Martin Deering said.

Sadie and Edwin said good-bye to their friends and went out to the car. Edwin pulled out of the parking lot and turned toward her home.

"Are you tired?" he asked. "You seemed awfully quiet this evening."

"Mostly thinking," Sadie said.

"Care to tell me what about?"

"Roz mostly, and how the flap over the filmmaking will make her feel." Briefly, she told Edwin about her conversation with Roz that morning.

Edwin sighed. "She's right, in a way. I remember when the accident happened, but I confess I hardly thought about it this week, even when people were talking about the movie. Of course, it was fifty years ago, and I suppose no one much younger than us remembers very much about it. Most of the people connected to the opera house are younger, and they're very enthusiastic about tying local events in with the film crew's presence and the premiere next spring."

Sadie chuckled. "Makes me feel old. Was 1965 really that long ago?"

"I'm afraid it was. And a lot of people might not put it together that the young man who died was Roz's brother."

She nodded. "Especially people who've moved to Silver Peak since then."

"I don't think it would do much good to go around and clue everyone in," Edwin said.

"Heavens, no. I can just see Troy Haggarty doing a feature story on the old film, though. What if he dredged up the whole thing, accident and all, and put it on the front page of the *Sentinel*, without ever realizing who Mike was?"

"I can see how that might upset Roz," Edwin said.

"She'd be devastated." Sadie was silent for a moment, thinking about it. "I suppose we could tell Troy to make sure he avoided that very thing. Or would that backfire? I mean, why call his attention to it if he's blissfully unaware?"

Edwin frowned and shook his head as he turned onto Sadie's road. "Troy's a journalist, and a good one. He'll work this movie company story for all it's worth, and it wouldn't be fair to ask him not to."

"Maybe we should just tell him right up front how damaging it could be to sensationalize the accident."

"I'll have a word with him if you'd like. I could caution him to be sensitive about that angle." Edwin looked over at her, his eyebrows raised in question.

"That might be best. Don't give the impression that you're trying to censor him, but call on him to treat the family with respect."

"Troy's a good fellow," Edwin said. "I think he'll understand. And as you said, if no one tips him off, he could unintentionally cause a lot of pain." After a moment's silence, he said with more confidence. "Yes, I'll talk to him. Tomorrow if I can."

"Of course you remember Mike?" Sadie said.

"Sure. Wasn't he a senior that year?"

"Yes, he'd just graduated. He was quite a bit older than Roz."

Edwin nodded. "I know everyone from school was very upset by it. But I still think this new film project can be good for the town if no one lets it become a dark, gloomy cloud hanging over Silver Peak."

"Yeah, I agree. But Roz... I'll be there for her if she needs me." Sadie had given her promise that morning under pressure from her friend, but now her determination grew. She would put the unanswered questions about Mike's death to rest for Roz.

As Edwin drove higher up the mountain toward Sadie's house, she noticed a glow in the sky that seemed to originate at some point beyond her house.

"What's that?" She pointed.

Edwin peered ahead. "I don't know. It's the wrong direction for the moonrise."

"Could it be a fire?"

He said nothing, but drove up her driveway and parked in front of the house. Both of them got out of the car and hurried to the side lawn.

"It's some kind of aircraft," Sadie said uncertainly. "I saw a blinking light."

"It's steadier now," Edwin said. "But it's not moving the way a plane would."

"A helicopter?" Sadie hazarded.

"Can't be. It's not that far away, and there's hardly any wind. We'd hear a chopper for sure."

"I think it's over Milo's pasture." Sadie couldn't look away from the eerie illumination. The light reflected off the clouds, but the object from which it seemed to emanate sank slowly toward the horizon.

"Is it landing?" Edwin asked, his eyes still fixed on the blinking lights. The flying object lowered out of sight and then rose again to where they could see at least two distinct lights on it blinking. Edwin and Sadie turned and stared at each other.

"Okay, what is that thing?" she asked.

He shook his head slowly. "I haven't the faintest idea."

A Note from the Editors

We hope you enjoyed *Mysteries of Silver Peak*, published by the Books and Inspirational Media Division of Guideposts, a nonprofit organization that touches millions of lives every day through products and services that inspire, encourage, help you grow in your faith, and celebrate God's love.

Thank you for making a difference with your purchase of this book, which helps fund our many outreach programs to military personnel, prisons, hospitals, nursing homes, and educational institutions.

We also create many useful and uplifting online resources. Visit Guideposts.org to read true stories of hope and inspiration, access OurPrayer network, sign up for free newsletters, download free e-books, join our Facebook community, and follow our stimulating blogs.

To learn about other Guideposts publications, including the best-selling devotional *Daily Guideposts*, go to Guideposts.org/Shop, call (800) 932-2145, or write to Guideposts, PO Box 5815, Harlan, Iowa 51593.

Find more inspiring fiction in these best-loved Guideposts series!

Sugarcreek Amish Mysteries

Be intrigued by the suspense and joyful “aha” moments in these delightful stories. Each book in the series brings together two women of vastly different backgrounds and traditions, who realize there’s much more to the “simple life” than meets the eye.

Miracles of Marble Cove

Follow four women who are drawn together to face life’s challenges, support one another in faith, and experience God’s amazing grace as they encounter mysterious events in the small town of Marble Cove.

Secrets of Mary’s Bookshop

Delve into a cozy mystery where Mary, the owner of Mary’s Mystery Bookshop, finds herself using sleuthing skills that she didn’t realize she had. There are quirky characters and lots of unexpected twists and turns.

Patchwork Mysteries

Discover that life’s little mysteries often have a common thread in a series where every novel contains an intriguing mystery centered around a quilt located in a beautiful New England town.

Mysteries of Silver Peak

Escape to the historic mining town of Silver Peak, Colorado, and discover how one woman’s love of antiques helps her solve mysteries buried deep in the town’s checkered past.

To learn more about these books, visit Guideposts.org/Shop